THE SECRETS WE KEEP

Florida Sheriff Deputies
Murder Mysteries

THE SECRETS WE KEEP

Florida Sheriff Deputies Murder Mysteries

Angela Jarvis

ABSOLUTELY AMAZING eBOOKS

ABSOLUTELY AMAZING eBOOKS

Published by Whiz Bang LLC, 926 Truman Avenue, Key West, Florida 33040, USA.

For information contact:
Publisher@AbsolutelyAmazingEbooks.com

ISBN-13: 978-1945772993 (Absolutely Amazing Ebooks)
ISBN-10: 1945772999

Three people may keep a secret, if two of them are dead.

- Benjamin Franklin

DEDICATION

In doing research for this book, I was heartbroken by the very things I had to research. The articles I read that explained the everyday life and treatments children often received in asylums that were meant to take care of them, was terrifying.

These children were thrown away by their parents and families for simple illnesses or common childhood behaviors such as bedwetting, and as a mother, I cannot fathom sending my children away for anything, much less things such as these.

The images that accompanied these articles were haunting. The tiny faces of children that would never know a mother's love or a father's protection, were almost at times too much to look at.

This book is dedicated to all those children who ever felt lost, alone, abandoned, or unwanted.

I wish I could've helped you. I hope you have found peace in death's slumber that you didn't know in life.

You are not forgotten...

THE SECRETS WE KEEP

Florida Sheriff Deputies
Murder Mysteries

PROLOGUE

The eerie silence of the abandoned hospital was deafening. It had stood empty for the better part of 30 years and decay was present everywhere.

Careful not to trip on the debris that lay strewn about, teens Logan and David navigated the corridors carefully.

Armed with only a flashlight, a fancy new camera, and a small hand-held recorder, their mission was to find some ghosts. They were amateur ghost hunters, but were hoping to gain the respect of other, more experienced hunters in the area. This was the reason they had snuck into this place. It was off limits to everyone, as the numerous *No Trespassing* signs reiterated. There had been several ghost hunting groups that had tried to get permission to come out here, only to be denied by the elusive owner of this place. No one knew who owned it because it was under the management of a corporation, and they would not give out that information. Of course, it had been easy to sneak in here, even though there was a security guard at the gated entrance. They simply waited until he was engrossed in a basketball game on a small TV in the guard shack. When they were positive they wouldn't be caught, they snuck under the fence. The spot they crawled through was hidden by some brush so you couldn't see where it had been pushed up.

If they could manage to get some good evidence here, they might be asked to join one of the more established paranormal groups. Maybe they could even form their own.

A small tapping noise could be heard coming from the room that used to be the infirmary/morgue area.

They both looked at each other, and David mouthed, "Let's go."

Cautiously, they proceeded down the long hallway. Sounds of dripping water grew louder, and every few steps a drop or two would hit one of them in the face or shoulder. It seemed it was unavoidable.

Just as they reached the door to the infirmary area, the tapping ceased. Both boys stopped dead in their tracks. They waited a few seconds before continuing inside the double doors. Slowly pushing them open, they stepped inside, and were immediately enveloped in darkness except for the dim beam of the flashlight.

Slowly Logan swept the flashlight to the left and then around the room to see if the source of the tapping could be found. Panning half way around, he almost dropped the flashlight. He let out a small panicked yell. There, on an exam table, was a skeleton.

David slapped him on the back and laughed. "Damn man, you scared the hell out of me. By the way, you scream like a girl"

"I don't scream like a girl. It looked like a dead person."

"It's probably a left over from that haunted house they had out here a few years back before the owner got a stick up his ass and wouldn't allow it anymore."

Logan grinned at his own foolishness. Of course, he remembered it now. He had wanted to come but his mom wouldn't let him. He had been "too young" according to her for that kind of scare. Releasing a nervous laugh, he walked around the table.

"Man, they sure make these things look real. It has jewelry on and everything." Logan explained thinking that was odd.

"It's supposed to look real to scare people dummy. It scared you didn't it?" David teased. He snapped a couple of pictures with their new camera, and moved across the room to the vaults they kept dead bodies in until they could be transferred out to funeral homes, or whatever they did with them.

Logan wondered if the bracelet was real. It couldn't hurt to take it and find out. Whoever put it there obviously didn't want it, and it could bring a few bucks at the pawn shop. He slipped it off the skeletons wrist when suddenly they heard the tapping sound again, only this time it was louder. It startled him and he dropped the bracelet down one of the drain holes in the table. Dammit!

'Would you quit playing with that thing? Come on, the sound is in another room now. Let's go," David suggested leaving the room.

Logan followed him chasing whatever imagined ghost was out there.

Neither realized the skeleton they just found was real. It was not a leftover Halloween prop.

Once, it had been a teenager, just like them.

CHAPTER I

The bright sunshine contradicted Dagan Murphy's mood as he climbed out of his pickup truck. He had to park in a spot for visitors because some rookie had taken his usual space. You picked the wrong day kid, he thought to himself as he walked across the lot.

He hadn't slept the last two nights and was grouchy as hell. His boss had already been calling his phone looking for him and it wasn't even eight a.m. yet. He was certainly not in the mood for her crap this early.

No sooner had he walked in the front door of the station, she was yelling out for him to get in her office. Like a bull facing a matador waving a red cape, he raged across the office floor and everyone that noticed him steered clear of him.

He slammed the door closed as he entered her office.

"Was that really necessary?" she asked in a much calmer voice that he expected. He dropped down in the chair that sat in front of her desk and slumped down a bit. Leaning his head on the back of the chair, he let out a slow breath of air.

Sheriff Alice Taylor raised her eyebrows momentarily then asked, "Is your temper tantrum over?"

Picking his head up, he looked her directly in the eye and responded, "I'm having a bad week, not throwing a tantrum. If we can get on with whatever reprimand you think I need, then I can get back to work. After all, it is what you pay me for."

Looking as if she wanted to say one thing, and then changing her mind she responded quietly, "Putting our

1

professional business aside for a moment, I know why you're having a rough week, and I'm sorry. I called your mom last night and she was having a rough time too.

Have you spoken to her?"

"No." He hesitated a moment. "I haven't had time to go by there. Tracy broke it off Monday night. I've been trying to figure some things out since then."

"I had no idea. That on top of the anniversary of Rachel's disappearance would make for a pretty crummy week."

"Yeah, no kidding," he said running his fingers through his hair.

Her eyes brimmed with tears, then she sucked in her breath and felt it better to get on with the work issues at hand. "Now, about you wasting department resources which are already next to nothing, on this old case. It's not even in our jurisdiction." Before she could finish her explanation, Dagan interrupted.

"I just have a feeling that it's related to Rachel's case. I'm this close to connecting the two together," he explained holding two fingers about an inch apart. "There are a couple others that fit the profile too."

Sighing, she responded with as much understanding as she could. "Dagan, let it go. Please. This is the last time I'm asking nicely. I have people that I have to answer to as well."

They sat staring each other down.

"Whatever." He stood and walked out.

"Don't slam..." too late, "...the door," she finished to no one.

Taking her glasses off and laying them on her stack of paperwork, she rubbed her eyes. If Dagan had been anyone else, she would have fired him for such insubordination a long time ago, but she loved him too much and because of that love, she understood him. She was his mother's best friend, and his godmother.

She supposed she overlooked a lot where he was concerned when she should be harder on him than the rest. She didn't have children of her own, which was probably a good thing since she had three failed marriages. She was glad there weren't any children to suffer through that, but because she never had any of her own, she had always thought of Dagan and Rachel as close as she would ever get. Rachel's disappearance had affected her deeply and broken her heart, but it was nothing compared to what Dagan's parents, Sam and Maureen, had suffered.

Sam, who had also been a deputy, kept looking for his little girl right up until the day his lung cancer wouldn't allow him to, and on his deathbed made Dagan promise to never stop looking for her. What started as a promise to a dying father, had turned into a cruel, unending torture for Dagan. She knew that is not what Sam intended for his only son, and she had said as much to Dagan and Maureen.

Maureen agreed. Dagan did not.

Rachel had been missing for ten years. She would have been twenty-seven in a few months if she were still alive. Alice knew in her heart, and because of her experience as a law enforcement officer, that Rachel being alive was not very likely in the realm of possibilities. Add to that, the fact they had never been able to find her body to give her a proper burial, and it was a heartbreaking nightmare for everyone involved.

Instinct told her he would not give up working on the other cases that he thought could be connected to his sister's disappearance.

So be it. As long as he did it on his own time and not the departments.

She was having to account for every minute her deputies spent on patrol because of departmental cutbacks. Dagan was making it hard because even though he was a detective, he was not assigned to work cold cases. She could make it so he was, but he was putting too much of his time, on the clock and off, into it. That boy needed a life that didn't revolve around his missing sister. Chances were though he would never stop looking, and therefore it might be better to give him free reign to do it.

Who knew the right answer?

He had already lost a wife, one his family absolutely adored, now a girlfriend of almost a year.

She could sense a storm brewing in that boy's life. She only hoped it would wash away the bad and bring something good to him.

CHAPTER 2

Pushing away from the desk to stretch his arms above his head, Dagan decided to call it a day since it was already after five. The county of Washington was not the largest in the state, but it was pretty big. Though he worked in the City of Chipley, he lived in Oakville, about a twenty-minute drive from the station. He gathered some papers and files on his desk that he would work on at home and headed for the door. He thought about going by to see his mom. He was having a hard time dealing with his emotions, and he didn't know if he could handle hers too. Coward, he thought to himself.

Scanning the parking lot, he noticed most everyone else had already left and the next shift was filing in. A few of them called out to him and he exchanged waves and hellos.

He reached his truck and opened the door. A tsunami of hot air greeted him.

He had to stand outside the truck for a couple of minutes just so it would be possible to get in, and not steal his breath away. The inside of vehicles reached the boiling point in the hot Northwest Florida sun.

Finally, he could climb into the cab. He cranked up the AC wide open. He would be lucky if it cooled off by the time he reached home. At least he had AC. The patrol car he had to use earlier to go into Panama City Beach had none. It was the only car available and they had not gotten around to fixing it yet. It wasn't too bad as he had cruised along Front Beach Road. The ocean breeze was nice. He had noticed the crowds were dwindling after another hellacious spring break season that had kept a lot of the departments around here busy with plenty of overtime. Kids came from all over looking to have a good time, but often, ended up finding trouble when it could be so easily avoided.

He had never been on spring break. He had always been too focused on his career goals and didn't take any chances that could derail it. He had always wondered if his sister would have been among those kids. Chances are she would have tried, but he would have been right there looking over her shoulder, steering her clear of trouble.

Young girls did not know or seem to care about the dangers they faced on the beach and in the clubs every year.

That whole *it won't happen to me* mentality had led to countless drugged and drunken girls being raped. Thankfully for the police, stupidity knows no bounds. In the age of technology, kids like to record everything and put it on social media. That helped put quite a few of the young men who had committed these crimes behind bars. The city council had outlawed drinking on the beaches for the spring break months, but kids always found a way.

Of course, there were the bar and club owners complaining about lost revenue. He guessed underage kids' lives and wellbeing was nothing compared to the almighty dollar. Not all the kids were underage, but many of them were. There would never be a happy medium because the residents resented the kids making a mess on the beaches and leaving it. For a generation that constantly yelled and screamed about saving the environment, they had no desire to do so themselves when it came to partying and having a good time.

He loved going to the beach, but lived 45 miles from it in his little hometown of Oakville. Population

3014. 3015 if you counted the town's mascot, a mini horse named Apache.

There was only one red light, one café, and one convenient store/gas station. That is exactly why he loved it. Of course, there was a Super Wal-Mart just ten minutes down I-10 for all your shopping needs.

His Florida cracker style house was five miles off the highway situated on forty acres of land. His nearest neighbor was a good 10 miles away. He had never felt lonely surrounded by the pine forest, and he loved the peace and quiet. There were plenty of forest critters to keep him company along with his pair of golden retrievers Kojak and Columbo. He had found the brothers abandoned on the side of the highway, wet and dirty, covered in fleas, and half starved. He took them home, cleaned them up and fed them. They had been his constant companions ever since.

His phone jangled in the cup holder of the console. He looked at the caller ID and it read MOM. He might as well get it over with so he answered it.

"Hey mama." He answered with the familiar term of southern endearment.

"Hi Dagan. It's good to hear your voice." Her voice sounded broken, as if she had been crying.

"Sorry I didn't call earlier, it's been a long day. I'm just now getting home."

"Oh, I was going to see if you wanted to have supper with me. I made your favorite, lasagna." She sounded so sad it made his heart twist.

"Sure mama. Let me grab a quick shower and let the dogs out and then I'll be there. Give me about thirty minutes."

They said their goodbyes and hung up. He felt like such a jerk for not calling her sooner. He had lost a sister, but she had lost a child. That was something he couldn't comprehend. Now that his dad was gone too, she was all alone in that four bedroom, three and a half-bath monstrosity of a log cabin Dad built when he was a baby.

As he pulled into his drive, he could see "the boys" as he liked to call them, through the picture window in the living room. He had started leaving the blinds open so they could see out, after they tore one set down when they were only six months old. Brats, but he loved them.

Suddenly they disappeared, and he knew they would be at the front door. He was immediately attacked and licked in the face as he entered the house. He couldn't help but laugh. He wished everyone was always that happy to see him.

"Down," he instructed. They immediately obeyed the command and followed him into the kitchen. He opened the back door and they flew through into the huge expanse of yard. He whistled and they stopped to look at him.

"Don't go far. To the edge of the yard and that's it." They seemed to understand perfectly and went sniffing around to find just the right spot to do their business. The edge of the yard that butted up to the forest is where Kojak had chosen, and when he had finished he sat just staring out into the woods. He would turn and look at Dagan, then turn and look back into the woods. It seemed almost as if he was confused.

"Kojak, come." Looking once more at Dagan, then into the forest, he finally came running back to the porch.

"Did you see a deer or coon buddy?" Dagan asked. He patted the dog on the head and led them back inside to feed them. He poured their food, and then headed upstairs to take a shower.

Suddenly he was starving, and the thought of his mama's lasagna made his mouth water ensuring the shower would be a quick one.

CHAPTER 3

"Hey man, did you hear the latest?" Deputy Tyler Ford asked Dagan as he walked in the next morning.

"No, what?"

"Word is that a couple of kids found human remains in the old Oakville Asylum. I figured you'd be interested since you live out that way."

"I'll be sure to check into it."

"Might be just some old bum that wondered in for shelter and ended up dying there."

"Could be, but you never know."

"Wade Jeter is lead on it, so have fun. We all know how he feels about you," Ford said with a chuckle.

"He doesn't worry me. He's still mad because he didn't get the baseball scholarship to FSU and I did. He just didn't have the grades."

"Not to mention, he thinks you stole his girl."

"Dani was never his girl. She never so much as batted an eye at him. His problem was he thought he was God's gift to women."

"In case you haven't noticed, he still does."

Captain Taylor opened her office door and interrupted their conversation by telling Dagan she needed to talk to him.

Pushing back from his desk, he muttered, "Wonder what I did this time?" He set his coffee mug down on his desk a little too hard and sloshed some on the calendar leaving a stain. He sighed and grabbed a handful of tissues to blot it up. He threw them away and walked over to her office. He took a seat across from her and remained silent as she looked at something on her computer screen.

Looking up at him over the rim of her glasses, she said, "I see you're in a much better mood today."

"I guess I should apologize," he began red-faced from his actions yesterday.

She held her hand up stopping him from going further with his apology. "None necessary. We all have bad days, or weeks in your case."

He managed a smile. "Still, I am sorry."

"Alright, apology accepted. Now, the real reason I called you in here. I am reassigning you."

"What?" he asked incredulously. "I happen to like where I am and what I'm doing. If this is punishment for yesterday..."

Again, she stopped him mid-sentence, crossed her hands in front of her and placed them on her desk. "It's not! I should have worded it differently. You'll still work your regular shift and maintain your position as a detective, but I've decided to give you the leeway to work with the cold case unit too. I received word that some remains were found at the old asylum, you can start there. We don't have much yet except the bones look as if they have been there for quite some time. You can work this as both detective and to check cold files to see if any old cases fit."

"I thought Jeter was lead on this case?"

"He is, but two heads are better than one."

"Not when one is made from concrete."

"Yours or his?"

"Oh, you've got jokes today?"

"You forget, I've known you your entire life. I admit, I've always thought it was a bad idea, but after reevaluating everything, I'm sure you'll be an asset to them. You're skilled at finding minute details and who knows, maybe you can close some of these old cases around here and give those families some closure."

"You mean my family."

"If that happens, then all the better."

"Thank you," he said much too quietly for a man of his size. He realized he had once again benefitted from her being his godmother.

"You're welcome. Now get to work." Then she threw his own words from yesterday at his back as he walked out. "After all, it is what I pay you for."

He was glad she couldn't see the grin on his face as he walked back to his desk. Sitting down he was already strategizing in his head on what needed to be done. He knew at some point he had to go pay Jeter a visit. This would definitely ruffle his feathers. Dagan smiled just thinking about it.

"What's so funny?" Ford asked as he sat down on the corner of Dagan's desk.

"The look on Jeter's face when I tell him he has to work with me from now on."

"Well hell, I want to see this myself."

"This is going to be fun. Or hell. Either way I can work on my ... these old cases out in the open now."

"Congrats man, I know you've been wanting this for a while." Ford slapped him on the shoulder as he walked past him to his own desk

Dagan pulled up a folder he kept in a password-protected file on his desktop. It had all the cold case reports he had managed to find. He also searched and found the report on the new case of the remains found at the asylum to see if he could pick out any similarities. He wrote down the names and addresses of the boys who found the bones. He would go speak to them to hear their stories in their own words. Sometimes things got lost in translation from witness to paper. He had to stay one step ahead, because once Jeter found out that they were working together, he would throw up every roadblock he could just to screw with Dagan.

11

The Secrets We Keep

The names in the report didn't sound familiar to Dagan. David Penn and Logan Simms. The report showed their addresses were on Mulberry Street, a few houses apart. He just hoped they would be at home when he got there.

The good thing about living in a small town, most drives were short ones, but pleasant. A lot of retired folks could be seen sitting on their porches in swings or rocking chairs and waved as you went by.

Most people left their doors unlocked because you were somehow related through blood or marriage to most everyone in town, and the ones you weren't related to had known you all your life, therefore you didn't worry.

The local coffee shop, the Coffee Bean, was a gathering place for most people first thing in the morning, and a lot of the housewives in town liked to have lunch there with their friends to discuss the latest gossip. Since everyone knew everyone else, small towns harbored secrets. Feelings could run awfully deep, and sometimes those feelings were simmering right under the surface, kept at bay by the need for that secrecy. If you spoke to the right person, they could tell you everything you needed to know. This one was having an affair with that one, but who could blame him when he grew up seeing his daddy cheat on his mama, and with none other than the piano player down at the Methodist Church. Oh, and did you hear that so and so was going to jail for giving his wife a black eye when he thought she had talked to an imaginary lover outside the post office. It was all too ridiculous for him.

Most of the time.

Sometimes, it helped him get information he needed for a case. He then pretended to go right along with the whole *small towns, small minds* mind set.

12

He pulled into the middle-class neighborhood that had streets that were all named after trees. Mulberry was the one he was looking for. All the lawns were manicured nicely and the older, historic homes, were maintained beautifully. He was glad to see that some of the towns' history was being preserved.

124 and 128 Mulberry were on the same side of the street. He pulled into the driveway of the first. The sprinklers were going so he was very careful as he stepped out of the truck to stay on the concrete as he approached the door to ring the bell. It took a few seconds before a woman, who looked to be in her mid-forties, answered.

"Hello ma'am. I'm Detective Dagan Murphy with the Wilmington County Sheriff's Department. I need to talk to Logan Simms about his discovery the other day. Is he home?" He pulled out his badge and ID and showed it to her. She glanced quickly at it.

"He was until about fifteen minutes ago. He walked over to his friend's house. Is there anything I should be concerned about officer?" She put ridiculous emphasis on the word officer trying to sound sensual. Her eyes roved up and down giving Dagan the once-over.

"No ma'am. I am just following up with him and David Penn. I want to make sure they haven't remembered anything that could be significant to the case. No matter how small it seems, sometimes those are the things that could solve the case."

"Are they in trouble for trespassing?" she asked, leaning against the doorframe trying to show off her ample breasts.

"I am not sure about that. It really depends if the owner of the property wants to press charges."

"He's a good kid, makes good grades. He has never been in trouble in school or anywhere else for that matter. He just likes fooling around with that ghost

13

stuff." Again, she emphasized fooling around. He wanted to roll his eyes but suppressed the urge.

"You said he's at his friend's house?"

"Yes. Two doors down. The one with the dark gray roof."

"Thanks. You have a good day."

"You too."

Although he was walking away, she stood watching him go for a few seconds before finally closing the door. He wanted to tell her to be careful or she would wind up on the gossip's lips at the next ladies lunch.

He made the short drive two houses down and repeated the same process as before, only this time a man answered the door. He introduced himself and asked him if the boys were still here and if so, could he speak to them.

"This about that body they found the other day?" the man asked.

"Yes sir."

"I guess it's okay. Try my hardest to keep the boy out of trouble. It hasn't been easy since his mom died."

"He's not in any trouble that I'm aware of. I just want to see if they remember any details they might have left out of the report or have remembered since then."

He gestured for Dagan to come in. "I told him if I have to pay any fines I would take it out of his hide."

Dagan followed the man into a living room that was worn but clean. The man walked to the bottom of the stairs.

"David, you and Logan get your butts down here. There's a deputy that wants to talk to you." He turned sticking his hand and said, "I'm sorry, I am Phil by the way, David's dad."

"No problem."

"I didn't know whether to believe them when they come home telling that story. Especially when they are into all that horror stuff, scary movies and ghosts and such. He got that from his mama. I have never believed in that kind of thing."

"Me either. I can see how it would fascinate some people. Especially the young and curious."

"A bunch of hog wash if you ask me. You die. You go to heaven or hell, end of story. You don't float around trying to talk to the living or scare them." He plopped down into an overstuffed recliner about the time the boys came scrambling down the staircase.

"Hi boys. I am Detective Dagan Murphy. I just wanted to follow up with some questions about the other night."

"We told the other deputy everything, honest!"

"I'm sure you did, but sometimes we remember things a few days after something happens and our nerves settle down. It might not seem important at the time, but can actually be the one thing we need to solve a case."

"Oh," they said in unison.

"Why don't you start out by telling me exactly what happened Saturday night from the beginning? Don't leave anything out even if it seems silly or insignificant."

They looked at each other, then Logan spoke first.

"We've been hearing things at school. You know, about the old asylum being haunted. We wanted to take our new equipment out over there to see if it worked."

"New equipment?"

"A new digital recorder for capturing EVPs. That's electronic voice phenomenon. Ghost voices you can't hear with your normal hearing." We also had a new full spectrum camera that can be used for several different things. Mostly we used the infrared setting that night

15

to try and pick up anything that might manifest itself. We know that there's a security guard but we were told by some guys at school if you waited until 8:30 that he would settle down to watch some TV show he likes and you can just sneak through an opening in the fence."

"So, these other kids, what do they do out there? Were there any out there that same night."

"We don't want to get anyone in trouble." Both boys were looking at each other, then Dagan nervously.

David's dad spoke up. "You don't mind getting yourself in trouble, do ya?"

"No one is in trouble ok? I just need to know because the more people that were out there, the more contaminated the crime scene could be," Dagan reassured them.

"There was nobody out there that night but us. As far as what the others do out there, we've just heard rumors. Stuff like Satan worship and séances. We don't do that kind of stuff though." This time it was David who had spoken.

"Ok, fine. What next?" Dagan asked.

Logan continued, "We made it under the fence and into the building. We went from floor to floor. Everything was quiet until we heard a tapping noise. It sounded like it was coming from the next hall, which is down the same hall the morgue used to be. We both thought it would be a good place to get some EVP's and check out what the sound was. We went down there and that's where we found the skeleton. We thought it was a fake left over from a few years ago when they had a haunted house there."

"Yeah that's why you screamed like a girl, because you thought it was fake," David teased his friend.

"Shut up man! When we got ready to leave, I snapped a couple of pictures. I just thought if it was a

real person, the pictures would be kind of cool to have."
He didn't dare mention the bracelet he tried to take.

"I'm glad we didn't think that while we were still there. Ghosts are cool, but a real dead person, that's gross," David chimed in.

Dagan was trying to contain a smile. "Okay. How did you two get out?"

"The same way we got in. The guard was asleep by then."

"So, nothing else sticks out about the place or that night?"

"No sir. You can see the pictures we took if you want to." Logan offered.

"You can email them to me at this address." He gave boys one of his business cards. "Those numbers on there are my cell phone and the office number. If either of you think of anything else that you think would be useful, don't hesitate to call me."

"We won't," they said in unison.

Dagan thanked David's father and said he would see himself out. The man looked grateful he wouldn't have to move from his recliner and went back to flipping through a magazine.

He decided his next step would be to ride out and look around the old asylum. He wasn't a bit worried about finding any ghosts, but he did wonder who else might be lurking around in the old dilapidated building. It had to be someone willing to leave behind the remains of a person. But why there?

There had been rumors of the buyer turning it into a hotel resort with a fancy golf course. Maybe a local was trying to scare off the developer from building anything there. Some of these small-town folks didn't take well to progress and change. Maybe whoever left it there was long gone by now. Who knew at this point?

He would find out one way or another. If he had his way, no other family would ever have to endure the hell he and his family had been through since that fateful day 10 years ago that had changed his life forever.

CHAPTER 4

Dagan pulled up to the security guard house and after about thirty seconds, blew his horn to get the guards attention. He had been so engrossed in whatever was on the small TV he was watching, he hadn't even heard Dagan pull up. There's an employer getting his money's worth, he thought sarcastically. It's kind of hard to miss a full size pickup truck pulling up to a gate in the middle of nowhere.

He showed his badge and ID to the guard who then pressed the button to open the gate and allow him entrance.

The asylum was about a mile or so down the road, but couldn't be seen from here for all the trees lining both sides of an old bridle path that had long ago been graveled.

The road was flanked on both sides by huge oak trees that were draped with Spanish moss. It gave the drive a serene vibe. Eventually, the driveway opened to a monstrosity of a decaying remnant of long ago. The isolation of this place when it had been operating had to be terrifying to the children who had been abandoned here for any number of reasons. Any direction you looked, there was nothing to see in the distance but forest.

He parked in the semicircular drive in front of the building and got out to stand momentarily studying the building. The sole purpose of this place was to be a mental asylum. The architects of the day must have thought if they made it seem a pleasant place, it would somehow make up for the atrocities that would be endured on the inside.

His Aunt Pearlie Joe had worked here back in the late seventies and early eighties until they closed. He had heard her tell how she gave every attention to the patients, but for everyone she helped, there were ten more being neglected. She just couldn't do it all on her own, and most others who worked here didn't care. These were the forgotten children, the embarrassments to their families, disappointments, and burdens of society. They were dropped off here, and never mentioned again by those who were supposed to love them.

The hellhole disguised as an antebellum southern mansion seemed as sad as the lives of those who once resided here. Four massive pillars lined the front, covered in cracks and moss. A stately veranda swept the entire length of the front, and the second and third floors boasted of open-air porches for those who had suffered from tuberculosis and needed the fresh air, or so the doctors thought at the time.

Even though there was beauty in the structure, he couldn't help feeling a sense of foreboding. That was in the bright light of day he felt that way. Those boys had been brave to come out here at night. Dagan carried a gun for a living and was not at all sure he would venture here after sunset.

The massive double front doors, that were at least nine feet tall, were made from solid pine. Trying the doorknob, he was very surprised to find it unlocked. The doors made an awful unearthly groaning sound that could have come straight from the bowels of hell. Some bad ass cop you are, he thought as his first instinct was to turn around and leave.

A cool breeze blew past his head and neck. His imagination was going to great lengths to mess with him because he could imagine his sister's voice whisper "stop being a scaredy-cat." As if his head was on a pivot, he looked around to realize there was a breeze coming through the open front doors. He smiled and mentally called himself a dumbass. Of course, the mind always played tricks on people in these places, and he was no exception. He should be though. He had seen one too many scary movies. Common sense and a level head should always prevail when working any case.

Even this one.

The reception area was probably at one time a rather warm and inviting place for patients and their families.

A perfect façade to what lay ahead beyond the sweeping grand staircase. There wasn't much left anymore, just a built-in reception desk and a couple of broken, overturned chairs that were now home to spiders.

On either side of the staircase, were several rooms that had been used for administration purposes and doctor offices. Behind the staircase, the hallway split to the left and right. The signs on the wall indicated a solarium to the left and a cafeteria to the right.

He returned to the head of the staircase and ventured up. The stairs creaked as he made his way to the second floor. The first room he came to must have been a playroom. An immense feeling of sadness overcame him. There, in the midst of a once brightly painted room, were toys scattered about. He bent down and picked up a teddy bear that had been tossed aside many years ago and sat it upright in the corner.

The ever-present Florida palmetto bug, A/K/A cockroach, crawled onto his hand from the teddy bear. He shook his hand to fling it off. He left the playroom and continued down the hall.

It seemed the other rooms on this floor were all patient rooms. They were mostly empty, a few having rusted bed frames still in them, but nothing else.

21

He found a smaller staircase that led up to the third floor. According to the reports he had read, this is where he would find the morgue/infirmary where the remains had been discovered. He was halfway up the stairs when the sound of a door slamming caused him to jump.

He stood still and listened.

Silence.

It was probably just the wind. There were a lot of broken windows for the wind to come through causing a door to be blown shut.

He continued walking up and this time he heard footsteps. Reaching the top, he turned slowly pulling out his gun. Someone else must be in the building. He stood there for two or three minutes waiting to hear the steps.

Again, silence.

Damn this place was unnerving. He holstered his gun and finally found the room he was looking for at the end of the hall. The walls on this floor were filled with graffiti. That is, the ones that the paint was not peeling off of in massive chunks. Someone had a sick sense of humor with pictures of the devil eating children, and a pit of fire with people trying desperately to get out, being two of the largest paintings that were intact indicating they must be recent.

There were writings too that were disturbing. The least of which was "if you want to know why children are this way, cut one open and find out."

What in the hell was wrong with people?

To get to the morgue, he had to walk through rows of old dilapidated hospital beds that gave off an eerie feeling. How many had suffered in this very room? How many children lay in those beds crying for their parents who would never know of their suffering? God, what an awful place. He would be glad to get out of here.

Walking through a swinging door that didn't really swing anymore, he found what he was looking for. He pulled out a small flashlight to look around because there weren't any windows in this room for some reason to let the sunlight filter through.

There were three now defunct body bays where a child was held until next of kin was notified, that was if they had chosen to be notified. There was an old cemetery out back full of kids who never got to go home again, even in death. He supposed three should have been enough, but then he had heard stories of bodies being stacked up on the floor.

He found the autopsy table that had broken police tape lying on the floor around it. He used the flashlight to sweep from the top to the bottom of the table. It looked like any from its time he supposed. There were small drains every few inches to allow bodily fluids to drain out the porcelain slab.

As he was examining the table, his flashlight reflected off something shiny in one of the drains. The hole was too small to get it with his fingers and he had nothing to try and grab it with. It was shiny gold like a piece of jewelry.

He would have to come back out here to get it with a pair of pliers or tweezers.

Great! He didn't relish the thought of coming in here again, but work was work, and that could be an important piece of evidence. He wondered why the forensics team has missed it. Maybe the light had been wrong and they simply hadn't seen it. His gut told him it was important though. He would be back this afternoon with the proper tools to get it out. If all else failed he would use a hammer and break it open.

More quickly than he had entered, he made his way back out. He stopped briefly to tell the guard he would be back that afternoon and to make sure there were no "visitors" A/K/A trespassers.

He was headed back to the station but first he would stop by his house to let the boys out since he lived so close. Kojak had been acting strange lately. Every time Dagan let them out, he would sit on the edge of the property and stare off into the woods.

Never barking, never trying to chase anything, just staring. He had never been the more curious of the pair, so it was indeed strange behavior.

He pulled into the driveway and their keen sense of smell had them looking at him from the front window. As soon as he stepped from the truck they disappeared.

Opening the front door, they jumped around and started licking him. Always happy to see their master. He wished everyone felt that way about him.

He walked straight through to the back door and turned them loose. At first, they played a bit and then relieved themselves on a couple of bushes.

He was checking his email on his phone when he looked up to find Kojak sitting and staring into the woods. He walked over to him and said, "What ya looking at boy?"

He stared at Dagan with big brown eyes as if he was trying to communicate something to him. Dagan stepped into the woods and walked a few yards in looking around. He could see nothing and no one. The wind had suddenly picked up and there was a nice cool breeze blowing. Maybe Kojak was smelling something in the air, it was rather windy here most of the time. Maybe a dead animal too far away for human noses to smell, but a dog could smell up to eleven miles away and up to forty feet underground. He had learned this while training with some of the K9's at the academy.

Because of their sensibilities, dogs were often utilized as search and rescue amongst various other law enforcement agencies and the military.

"Come on Kojak, let's go back inside."

The dog reluctantly followed Dagan and Columbo back in. When they reached the door, he turned and stared toward the woods once more, and then at Dagan as if he was confused. This convinced Dagan to search the woods more thoroughly when he had a chance.

He locked up and headed back to the station. He still had to read over the reports for this case and compare his cold cases to see if anything could be pieced together.

He had a feeling this was not going to be an open and closed case, it was going to require digging, patience and persistence.

Lots of it.

CHAPTER 5

Preliminary reports on the bones found earlier in the week had come back and were in an envelope on Wade Jeter's desk. He wasn't the slightest bit curious as to what the coroner had to say. He had his own theories. He didn't share many of his thoughts with his co-workers. He found most of them to be too ignorant to consider anything outside the "box". In this small-town department, everything was black or white. Most of them could not ponder a thought above or below that line. The only one who could come close to his knack for the job was Dagan Murphy. He couldn't stand him, so he hated giving him that much credit. He had always considered him an arrogant jerk since high school.

Everybody in town thought he was a golden boy. He had perfect grades, good looks, the most beautiful girl in school who later became his wife, and a free ride to college. He sneered as he thought about that. He screwed up the marriage and got dumped, and what good did college do him? He came back here with a masters in criminal justice to work at a podunk sheriff's office.

If he had received that scholarship, he could have gone places, on to bigger and better things. But, here I am, stuck in Hicksville, USA. Soon though, everything will be alright. He had plans after all. Plans that would one day show everyone he was just as special as Dagan. He had even worked up the nerve to ask Dagan's ex old lady out. He snickered at that thought. She hadn't said yes, but he felt her softening every time he asked. He would show her what it was like to have a real man in her life. Murphy better damn well stay out of his way too. It would be a shame if he ended up missing like his little sister did all those years ago.

Sometimes he scared himself with his thoughts.

It was bad enough he had been brought in on this investigation. He had heard earlier today that he had been assigned to the cold cases unit but was also still responsible for his regular duties. Just one more thing that got under Wade's skin was Sheriff Taylor let Murphy do whatever the hell he wanted to do simply because she was his godmother. That guy could fall in a pile of shit and come out smelling like a rose.

Speak of the devil. He could see Dagan coming in the front door of the office. He headed straight for Wade's desk.

Dammit!

Dagan had a smug look on his face Wade would love to wipe off.

"Good morning partner," Dagan said with a huge smile.

"If you say so," Wade grumbled with his mouth set in a hard line. He never looked up from the papers he was pretending to read.

"Have you gotten any prelims back from the coroner?"

"No." Wade lied.

"Have you called and asked if they are ready?"

"No."

"Ok, well I guess I will. By the way, stop talking so much. It's annoying."

Wade watched Dagan walk away from the corner of his eye. God, he hated that guy. Wait until Dani finally accepted his offer for a date. That would send him over the top.

Serves him right. He had everything and threw it all away because he was obsessed with looking for his long lost sister.

What a pathetic loser. Wade just couldn't understand why he was the only one who could see it. He knew Dagan's family was well liked and respected around the area. Everyone at the department went on and on about how great a guy Dagan's father had been.

He must have not been too damn great, he couldn't find his own daughter. The corners of his mouth turned up into a smile. He quickly remembered where he was and quashed it.

There would be enough time later for gloating. He would make sure when that time came, Dagan would be there to see it, front and center.

CHAPTER 6

agan wanted to slam the phone down he was so pissed, but pressing the end button on a cell phone did not give one the same satisfaction. Dropping it on his desk, he shook his head, and tossed his pen across the top of the desk.

Wade had outright lied to him. The coroner, Bill Walters, had sent the prelim report over this morning.

"So, this is how it's going to go? Two can certainly play that game." He had to explain to Bill why he had called and requested another copy to be sent via fax.

Bill had known both Dagan and Wade since high school. He had been an assistant coach for the baseball team. He knew what a jackass Wade could be.

"Some things never change," he had said to Dagan during their conversation on the phone.

"That's the truth." He thanked him and hung up.

He crossed the room with long strides and waited by the fax so it wouldn't "accidentally" be misplaced or any other excuse people in this office could come up with. Nobody here really liked Wade, but there were a few who tried to stay on his good side by kissing his butt.

It wasn't long before the quiet hum of the fax machine could be heard getting ready to process the report from Bill. The small computer readout window indicated that there would be six pages total. He made sure to count them as each one took its turn rolling out into a gray tray on the side of the machine.

Gathering them, he made his way to his desk with a brief stop at the coffee pot on his way. Not that the stuff these guys brewed everyday should be called coffee. Burnt motor oil would be a better representation. Still, it was better than nothing.

Finally taking a seat, he began to read the report. The first page was just a cover page so he pushed it aside.

The bones were female ranging in age from fifteen to twenty-one. The skeleton was fully intact without even the smallest of bones missing. Her height was five feet seven inches and she had more than likely weighed about one hundred twenty pounds. There was no indication of any previous breaks or fractures, and all her teeth remained intact and showed previous dental work. That was good, they could compare dental records, when they could get any indication as to who it could be.

Suddenly, an unpleasant thought popped into Dagan's head. A trickle of sweat formed and ran down the back of his neck, even though the air condition was steadily humming and keeping the office quite cool. It caused him to shiver.

The profile for this person fit his sister. The height, weight and age range all fit.

He pushed away from his desk and felt a heavy brick in his stomach. Could this be her? Had she been under his nose all these years? He forced his thoughts to stop the direction they were headed. There were several missing people who could fit the profile description.

These remains had been placed there recently. The asylum closed in the early eighties and there had since been two owners, one of which ran a haunted house out there several years back at Halloween. Surely the remains would have been found before now.

Why would someone place the remains there now? Was whoever responsible feeling remorse, or trying to get caught?

Dagan needed some air. Suddenly remembering he needed to go back out to the asylum to retrieve whatever he had seen in the drain, he headed down to Raquel Johnson's office. She was the IT tech and had a small toolbox that contained different pairs of tweezers. He had seen her use them on numerous occasions repairing things around the office. She wasn't in her office but Dagan decided to borrow them anyway. He knew she wouldn't mind. She had been throwing subtle hints at Dagan about going out for months now.

He put them in his pocket and told the sheriff's secretary where he was going in case anyone asked for his whereabouts.

Not really looking forward to returning to the asylum, but needing that bit of evidence had him feeling conflicted. He didn't really believe in ghosts and all that hocus pocus, but that place was about a twenty on the creepy scale of one to ten. The dead couldn't hurt anyone, the living was another matter.

Arriving at the entrance to the asylum, the guard recognized him from earlier and buzzed him through. He was filled with trepidation as he rode up the driveway but soon the stately mansion came into view once more. He knew this place had to have been architecturally beautiful in its day. That was before cracked and broken windows, peeling paint, and overgrowth of bushes and trees that hadn't seen a trim in a long time had taken over. Dagan had seen a few pictures of it when it had been newly built. Even in those old black and white photos, you could almost see the color in the roses that lined the gardens out front and around the now dried up water fountain. He remembered the nurses in the heavily starched uniforms that had to be uncomfortable as hell, standing in a row alongside doctors, all with blank expressions on their faces. He though it odd he could remember that picture. Where had he seen it before? It didn't really matter now, those people were long gone, and this place barely resembled itself from the picture.

Climbing out of the truck, he noticed there was a storm building in the east. Of course, Murphy's Law states there simply must be a terrible storm when one is visiting a "haunted" asylum. He made sure he had his flashlight and started to the front doors.

There was enough light in the lobby that the flashlight wasn't necessary. After going upstairs and down the hallway, it grew a bit darker so he turned it on as a precautionary measure. He could hear the sudden flapping of wings and knew he had probably disturbed some nesting mourning doves. They had flown out quickly leaving dust particles floating in the air. They were illuminated by the rays of his flashlight and seemed to be dancing as they fell downward. For some reason, as he passed the nurses station on the second floor where the patients' rooms were, he noticed papers scattered on the floor. He hadn't seen them earlier today and curiosity got the best of him. He walked around picking up a few and reading them. Tossed carelessly around were the pages of people's lives. Someone today could have a real strong case for abuse of the HIPPA laws. Of course, back then, such laws didn't exist. A lot of the papers were nasty and waterlogged and couldn't be read, nor could you tell who they belonged to. After all these poor souls suffered, this just made it seem worse.

He saw a file that had several papers hanging out of it that looked to be in reasonably good shape. He picked it up to thumb through it. In it, he found a paper that had a list of reasons that a child might be admitted to this place. He could hardly believe what he was reading. The top few had him shaking his head in disbelief.

Mania, fright by a dog, epilepsy, bed-wetting. There were even two girls admitted because they never got their periods. That was in and of itself lunacy! Were people really that barbaric that they would institutionalize their child for wetting the bed? There were even more reasons listed, along with papers that had treatments as well as cause and effects of said treatments, but he had to move on. He took those papers out of the file and folded them in half tucking them into the back of his jeans. Out of sheer curiosity, but at the same time, there were a few missing kid cold cases that were somehow indirectly tied to this place. It might be worth looking into at some point. He had almost forgotten his reason for being here in the first place.

He continued up to the third floor. Reaching the top of the landing he stopped. It seemed as if someone was following him. He heard footsteps again.

"Anybody there?"

Of course, no one answered. Then, as if it was muffled or far off in the distance, he thought he heard a child's giggle. It was a sound that made his blood run cold.

"Who's there?"

No answer.

"This is Sergeant Dagan Murphy with the Washington County Sheriff's office. Come out now. Show yourself." He demanded. In his peripheral vision, he thought he saw someone cross the hallway from one room to next and heard another giggle.

Dammit, it was probably kids in here playing hide and seek. He would have to run them out. He had told the guard to make sure no one got inside this building and he was damn sure going to get a piece of Dagan's mind when he saw him. He walked quickly down the hall to the room he saw the kid run into.

It was empty.

There was no other way out of the room except the way he had just come in. There was a small window about seven feet off the ground, but just enough to let in the natural light. It was much too high for a child or even a short adult to get to. The only thing in the room to stand on was an old sink, and it was against the wall opposite the window. Not to mention, he was on the third floor. He could have sworn this was the room, but maybe it was the next one down.

All seemed quite and still now. Maybe the brats got out somehow and ran off. Leaning his head down, he rubbed the back of his neck with his hand. It had been a long day. From this angle he could see the floor.

The dusty floor.

The dusty floor that had one set of footprints in the dust. His.

It took just seconds to process what that could possibly mean, and Dagan quickly walked down to the infirmary. He continued straight through to the morgue room and suddenly he was a man on a mission. It was to retrieve whatever was in that drain and get the hell out of here.

He reached the autopsy table and turned the flashlight towards the drain. It immediately reflected off the gold item. He took the long tweezers out of his pocket and used them to pull the object slowly out of the drain. It took two attempts but he finally got it.

It was a bracelet.

A bracelet he had seen before. One that the recesses of his memory was trying to make a connection with. He held the delicate piece in his shaking hands and turned the thin gold name plate over. Three initials were inscribed on it.

RMM

Rachel Marie Murphy. This bracelet belonged to his sister.

CHAPTER 7

agan felt as if his feet were glued to the floor. A cool breeze touched the back of his neck causing him to take a deep breath and finally turn around. He quickly turned and hurried out of the room, down two flights of stairs, and finally out the front doors. He didn't stop until he was sitting inside his truck, and then finally, he opened his hand to look again at the bracelet.

Had this been the jewelry David and Logan had talked about seeing when they found the skeleton? If so, had his sister been found at last? Why would she have been in that place and who the hell put her there?

Whoa, slow down Dagan, he thought to himself. First things first. He had to get a grip and treat this as he would any other case. Only it wasn't any other case.

A thousand questions and thoughts running through his mind, he could not think one single clear thought.

Years of worry, determination, searching, lost sleep, lost relationships, and this whole time she could have been right here. Not far, as the crow flies, from his very own house.

Plop, plop, plop. He looked up to find big fat raindrops beginning to fall.

The heavens were crying for him.

Crying for his dad, who died never finding his little girl, for his mom who still suffered, but most of all for Rachel, robbed of her life and future.

After several moments, his shaking ceased as he held up the bracelet. He had been an idiot by not following the proper evidence collection procedures. Now it had been contaminated with his fingerprints.

Damn. Maybe there was something that might still be recovered. He opened the center console and took an evidence bag out and placed the bracelet inside. Chances are it had been exposed to outside elements and there were no fingerprints at all. There might be traces of something that could be viable. Only time and the lab tech would tell.

He wanted to call his mom, but didn't want to upset her unnecessarily. He would wait until he knew exactly what he had.

He didn't really remember most of the drive back to the office. He barely made it through Alice's office door before he began pacing back and forth, and then finally plopping down in the chair nearest to him.

"What is wrong with you? You look like you've seen a ghost." She said teasing because she knew where he had been.

Without saying a word, he reached into his pocket pulling out the bag that held the bracelet inside, placing it on the desk in front of her.

"What's this?" she asked picking it up to examine it.

"Look close."

Twisting and turning the bag, she finally caught sight of the initials. She paled quickly as the blood drained from her face.

"Where ... where did you find this?" She asked in a whisper.

"The asylum. The same place as the remains were found. I spotted it this morning as I was looking around only I couldn't get to it without a pair of tweezers. I went back out this afternoon to get it."

"That's impossible," she said looking off kilter.

"What is?"

Taking a second before answering she finally responded, "I just mean after all this time, a piece of evidence that could help find Rachel ... It seems too good to be true."

"We can't be sure yet. I have her dental records. I am going to leave here and go straight over to Bill's office and have him do a comparison to see if they match up."

She looked as lost and sad as he felt.

"It could finally be over," She said more to herself than him.

"Maybe. Hopefully we'll know within the hour."

"Call me as soon as you know something," she directed quietly.

"Of course." He remained seated a few minutes more though it was obvious neither had anything else to say until Alice gathered herself enough to tell him to leave the bracelet with her, and she would see that it got to the lab for prints.

He walked out into the main office area and luckily most everyone had left for the day. He had to call Bill and ask if it was alright to come by with the hour being close to closing time. As he went to sit in the chair he could feel the papers he had stuffed in the top part of his waist band and reached back to grab them. He opened the top drawer of his desk, throwing them in to look at later.

He dialed Bill and found him still in his office. He asked to drop by and told him he would explain when he got there. He unlocked the bottom drawer of his desk and pulled out a file that had his sister's name on it. Inside were her dental records. He had kept this file just in case he ever needed it.

He needed it now.

He took his time driving to Bill's office not really in a hurry now to know the truth. What if it was Rachel? What if it wasn't?

He felt nauseous as he pulled into the parking lot and made his way to the front door. He found Bill in his office.

"Hey Dagan, what can I do for you?" Bill asked.

"I have some dental records that I want you to compare to the remains that were found the other day."

"Alright, let's have a look."

Dagan opened the file and handed the set of x-rays to Bill.

Bill's face registered shock as he read the name on a small sticker at the top of the x-rays.

"Dagan, these are ... I'm so sorry." Was all he could manage. "I'll get right on this. Are you staying here or do you want to follow me down?"

"I'll go. I feel like I need to be there."

"Of course. I understand."

Dagan was sure that he was taking the longest walk of his life, although it wasn't more than twenty yards or so. The hall just seemed to stretch out forever.

Bill held the door as they both entered the autopsy room. The remains were on a table covered up with a standard white hospital sheet.

Even though all that was left of this once full of life human was bones, it was still hard to look at. There was nothing left that would have even slightly resembled his sister.

The doctor began his examination comparing the teeth in the skull to those of the x-rays he had placed in the x-ray viewer. It took several minutes that to Dagan seemed like hours.

Bill pulled the glasses from his face and rubbed his eyes. With a huge sigh he said "these dental records do not match the remains. Though according to Rachel's x-rays, she had a few cavities and other dental work, this person had seven cavities and obviously never wore braces as she did."

The relief flooded through Dagan so forcefully he felt lightheaded. Relief for sure, but also disappointment. How was it possible to feel both at the same time? He wouldn't have to tell his mom Rachel was lost to them forever, but then again, he couldn't let his sister rest in peace beside their dad. He steadied himself on the edge of the table and said, "Thank you for doing this on such short notice." He extended his hand to shake his old coach's.

"That's not necessary son. You know I would give anything to help you put this to rest." He shook Dagan's hand and then patted his back with the other. Stating that he had some paper work to finish up, he left Dagan alone so he could collect himself.

Dagan stared down at the form on the table. "I will not stop until I find out who you are and give your family some closure." He pulled the sheet back up over the head.

He popped his head in Bill's office to say goodbye and thank him once more. They spoke about some other possibilities to identifying the remains and Dagan assured him he would be in touch.

Once he was back in his truck, he did something he hadn't done in years.

He cried.

He tried hard to keep the tears from flowing but couldn't. A good ten minutes later, he wiped his eyes on the sleeve of his shirt and cranked up.

Leaving the parking lot, he knew what his next stop would be. Mamas.

CHAPTER 8

The house was dark, except for the yellow beams coming from the kitchen window and one upstairs room.

Dagan pulled in behind his mother's Toyota and hesitated for a few minutes before getting out.

Was it really necessary at this point in the investigation to tell her about this? If she found out later he had kept it from her, there would be hell to pay, so he might as well get it over with.

He was trying to figure out the best way to broach the subject with her. He had found the bracelet, but the remains were not hers. Who was the poor soul back at the coroner's office and why did that person have his sister's bracelet?

Finally opening the door to climb out, he was greeted instantly by a buzzing wave of mosquitoes. He hurried to the front door to avoid a hundred stinging bites, he stopped briefly to knock to let his mom know someone was there, but used his key to enter refusing to be dinner for the little vampires.

She was coming down the stairs as he stepped inside. Judging from the towel around her hair and the pajamas, it was a good bet she had just taken a shower.

"Dagan, what are you doing here? Not that I'm not glad to see you." She smiled and kissed his cheek.

"Something happened today that we need to talk about and I wanted you to hear it from me first."

Concern swept her still beautiful features. Even with everything she had been through, she did not look her age. She was 55, and could easily pass for a woman ten years younger. "Is everything ok son?"

"Let's have a seat," he replied motioning towards the dining room table in the next room. "Some remains have been found out at the old asylum. Along with the remains, a bracelet was also found. It was Rachel's bracelet. Remember the gold one with her initials inscribed on it? I had her dental records compared to the remains and it's not her."

After a couple of seconds of letting the information digest, Maureen told Dagan, "It can't be Rachel's bracelet. I have hers in my jewelry box upstairs."

Now it was Dagan's turn to let things sink in. "Are you sure Mom? I remember the gold bracelet you and Dad bought her for her sixteenth birthday and this is it."

"I'm positive. I was just looking at it the other day." They both sat in a silence and stared at each other.

"She had a friend in school that had the same exact initials as she did. When they figured it out, they formed sort of a little bond. They didn't hang out much because the girl's parents were a bit odd and apparently the father had been in some trouble with the law, and well you know how your dad was about that sort of thing. Rachel felt sorry for her because her home life was so bad. Your sister asked if she could buy the girl the same bracelet for a Christmas gift and I couldn't say no. She had such a loving and caring heart."

"Do you remember her name?"

"Let's see. Her last name was Miller as I recall." Tapping her fingers on the table and concentrating she finally said, "Regina. That's it. Regina Miller."

"Good. I'll look into it and see what I can find out about her."

"I hope it's not her. I don't remember hearing anything about her going missing."

"I don't know. You said you have Rachel's bracelet and if she had one that was identical, who else could it be?"

"I pray it's not. Two beautiful girls just … gone." She had long ago given up hope of finding Rachel alive. She just wanted her baby back so she could put her to rest beside her father.

"I intend on finding out everything I can." Dagan stood up and walked around the table to hug his mom.

Not knowing what else to add, she offered to cut them both a slice of carrot cake. She prepared two pieces and poured two tall glasses of milk to wash it down with.

"Sorry to have to bring all this up mom. I just didn't want you hearing it anywhere else. I want you to know I haven't given up and I never will."

"I know Dagan, I love you for not wanting to give up on your sister. Please, don't let this consume the rest of your life. Did you hear what I just said? Your life. You have plenty left to live. There's really nothing we can do for Rachel anymore. If this investigation doesn't lead you to her, please for your own good and for mine, promise me you'll let it go" Her words were weighted by sadness.

"Mom…"

"Promise me Dagan."

"Ok, I promise."

"I love you son."

"I love you too."

Dagan hoped he could keep his promise, but he had bigger hopes that this would end it. Either way, he was going to have a hard time keeping the part of the promise that meant letting go.

CHAPTER 9

agan hurried his morning routine along. He wanted to get to the office early to follow up on his sister's friend as soon as possible. He had gotten home late from his mom's last night and fell asleep as soon as his head hit the pillow.

He arrived earlier than most at the office and it was quiet. That would give him time to work uninterrupted before the normal bustle of the day. He powered up his computer and signed in to the FCIC/NCIC, which was the Florida and National Crime Information Centers. He typed in Regina M. Miller. Several people by that name came up. Her birthday would be helpful and luckily there was only one female by that name with a birthdate that would put her the same age as his sister. He went on gut instinct and picked that one. It seems that she had been picked up a couple of times for prostitution. He printed out her rap sheet, which included her mug shot. She was petite brunette who looked older than she was. If she wasn't laying in the morgue, she was leading a less than upstanding citizen's life. Could this really be Rachel's friend?

Her last known address was in Panama City Beach, so it looked as if he would be making a trip there to find her. There were a few answers he hoped she would have, if she was even the right Regina Miller. He jotted her address on a small piece of note paper and stuffed it in his pocket. He didn't want to say anything to anyone else here in the department right now.

Dagan saw Wade enter the front door and he instantly developed a sour taste in the back of his mouth. He walked over and dropped a file on Dagan's desk.

"What's this?"

"Coroner's report."

"I don't' need it. I already spoke to him. As a matter of fact, I was there last night."

"Well aren't you Johnny-on-the-spot?"

"Someone has to be. No sense in dragging our feet."

"Why? It's not like the vic is going anywhere?" he answered with a smug smile.

Dagan wanted to wipe that grin from his face. Preferably with a chair.

"Tell me Wade, why did you go into this line of work? Was it because of your deep and abiding belief in justice, or the overwhelming need to help people and families in their times of crisis?"

That did the trick. The smile quickly faded off Wade's face, giving Dagan a small degree of satisfaction. Without saying a word, Wade turned to walk off.

"You forgot something," Dagan called out. But Wade continued towards his desk on the other side of the office. Dagan chuckled to himself.

Throughout the morning, Dagan could feel little daggers of pure hatred being tossed his way, but he chose to ignore it. He had enough to do without worrying about Wade being the ass he had always been.

He had explored several different databases and his own files that he had accumulated over the years, making comparisons to the remains. There just wasn't a lot to go on, but he was able to weed some of them out. He had three missing person reports that could possibly be a match. It was a start.

Deciding to go to Panama City Beach, he told the sheriff's secretary he was tracking down a lead, and to let the sheriff know when she came in. It was unusual that she wasn't here already, but he didn't keep tabs on her personal life. He grabbed his keys and headed out hoping he could locate Rachel's old friend.

~ ~ ~

Just like any other city, Panama City had parts of town that were better left unvisited by tourists and locals alike. If you were unfortunate enough to live in these areas, you had to keep your head on a swivel and what valuables you had on lockdown.

Violent crimes had supposedly declined in small percentages over the past couple of years according to statistics, but if you watched the nightly news, you'd never know it. Overall, it wasn't a bad place and there was a lot of fun to be had for adults and families alike, you just had to pay attention to your surroundings. Such is the way of the world these days he thought.

The address he had punched into his GPS had led him to the Driftwood Apartments complex. It was rundown, and the drab pea green color they were painted did nothing to add any curb appeal. There were several people sitting outside on their stoops or in lawn chairs, all of them watching him warily. The apartment was number 15 and on the second floor. There were only two floors, so he climbed the outside stairs on the side of the building to the top landing. Apartment 15 was closest to the stairs.

He knocked several times with no answer. It seemed quiet on the inside. He didn't hear a TV or radio. He knocked once more and after a few minutes went back down the stairs.

"Why you looking for Gina?" a young kid of about 15 asked.

"You know Regina Miller?"

"I know Gina. Might be short for Regina. Not sure what her last name is though. Never asked her and she ain't never said."

"Do you know where she might be?"

"Probably at work. Not everyone that lives here is on government checks you know."

Dagan tried to ignore the baiting. "Do you happen to know where she works?"

"She in some kind of trouble?" the kid asked wondering if he had said too much.

"None that I know of. She used to be friends with my sister when they were in high school. Just looking her up, making sure she's doing ok."

The kid took a few seconds deciding whether to believe Dagan. "She works at The Moonlighter."

"That a restaurant or a bar?"

"Nope. A strip club."

Dagan shouldn't be surprised. She did have a record of prostitution after all.

"Thanks." Dagan returned to his truck, typed in The Moonlighter in the GPS and followed the directions to the address.

How funny, he thought. All these years living this close to a place people came to party and he never once stepped foot into one of these places. Strangest of all, his first visit to one was to try and get information on his sister. His friends used to tease him when he was younger that he was whipped. They would invite him along on their trips to the clubs, but he had Dani at home and that had been enough for him.

He entered the dimly lit building. Once his eyes adjusted, he could see that there were very few customers at this time of the day. There was one lone dancer on stage, but he didn't know if it was Regina or not. She was a brunette according to her mug shot, but some women liked to dye their hair and the woman on stage was a blonde.

Taking a seat at the bar, he looked around. Not much to see. A couple of tables with some loners drinking and watching the girl on stage with not much interest. What a life. The bartender came over and asked what he could get him.

"I'm looking for Regina Miller."

"Look dude, I don't give out information on the girls."

Dagan reached into his back pocket pulling out his wallet that contained his badge. He showed him and then said, "I'm trying to make sure she's ok. She's a friend of my sister."

"I don't care who she is friends with..." the bartender began

"It's ok Bobby. I know him." A voice came from behind Dagan. He turned on his bar stool to come face to face with the girl from the mugshot.

"If you say so." He replied with a sour look and walked off to the other end of the bar.

"I'm Regina. I remember you. You're Rachel's brother. I heard you say that you wanted to see if I was ok. Why?"

"Can we go sit at a table and talk where we have a little more privacy?" he asked after noticing the bartender watching them out of the corner of his eye. They moved to a table in the far corner away from the stage and the music pumping through the sound system.

There was no easy transition into telling her what they found so he just put it bluntly. "A few days ago, there were some remains found. They belonged to a young girl. In recovery of the evidence, a bracelet was found. It was gold and had the initials RMM inscribed on it."

Her eyes widened and tears formed at the corners of her eyes.

Dagan continued, "My first thought was I had finally found Rachel. The coroner checked and it wasn't her. The odd thing was the bracelet that had her initials on it. That's why I thought it was her, but my mother has Rachel's bracelet. She told me about the one Rachel gave you for Christmas. I was making sure that the remains were not you."

Wiping the corners of her eyes, she told him "Rachel was the only real friend I ever had in that Podunk town. My home life was not all that great. My dad never could keep a steady job and my mama was a drunk. She didn't care what he did as long as he could bring home a paycheck for her to buy her beer with. When there was no work, they fought constantly. I was an only child so they barely noticed me. I always wanted a sister and Rachel was like that to me. She would loan me clothes and things to help me fit in better at school. It never worked though. The other kids still treated me like white trailer trash. When she gave me that bracelet for Christmas one year, I was in hog heaven. I had to hide it from my folks so they wouldn't try to pawn it for beer or a bill they needed to pay. I would leave it in my locker at school and wear it during the day. I got to school one morning, and someone had broken into my locker and taken it. I was devastated. Rachel and I tried to look on the arm of every girl at school that day, but we never found it."

"I'm sorry," he responded and he truly was for the life that this girl had to live. "I guess we found it finally, only we don't know who had it. You have no suspicions about who might have taken it?"

"No. I wish I did, and I wish more than anything I could help find Rachel. I really miss her."

"Me too. If you remember anything give me a call. Here's my card." He handed her a business card with his numbers at work, and his cell. They said goodbye, and he returned to his truck.

A thought suddenly occurred to him. If the bracelet was stolen at school, chances were more than great that it was another student around the same age as Rachel at the time. Could the remains be that of an old classmate of hers?

He did not remember any other kids going missing around that same time or even after, but then again, his family was so focused on finding his sister, everything else was a blur.

He certainly had his work cut out for him. He needed to research any other girls that disappeared around that time.

He prayed this would be the break he was looking for.

CHAPTER 10

agan called his mother after his visit to Regina in Panama City. He explained to her he needed to look through Rachel's old yearbooks, and she told him that they were packed away in the attic. For years, his mother had kept his sister's room just the way it had been the day she disappeared, including the dirty clothes in her hamper. After his dad died, she had decided it was time to put it to other use. It had been her way of moving on. She had cleared it out, giving the furniture and clothes to charity and then repainted it. It had become the library in tribute to the fact that she and Rachel had loved to read. Now it was complete with an overstuffed couch that sat by the window, which overlooked the back yard where Rachel had practiced her cheers, and the forest beyond where all of them had loved to take walks together as a family.

He let himself in and headed upstairs. In the hallway between his old room on one side and Rachel's on the other, there was a set of pull down stairs that led up to the attic. He remembered being a young boy trying to jump up and grab the ring that you used to pull them down and never being able to quite reach it. Now, it was barely a stretch for his tall frame.

Once he reached the top step, he felt around for the light switch on the right wall. As soon as the bulb was lit, it illuminated the dust particles floating around in the semi-darkness. He always thought it funny how people found attics scary. To him, it was a somber place where things of the past came to retire.

He had brought a battery powered lantern with him just in case the light bulb had blown or in this case, didn't give off enough light. He turned the switch on and the LED bulbs were quite bright.

He had to move some things around to find the boxes marked with his sister's name on them. His mom had explained the plastic storage containers had green lids, Rachel's favorite color. He finally spotted them towards the East end of the attic. There were several cardboard boxes directly in front of them that would have to be moved first.

He reached over to grab the top one and saw that his aunt's name was written in permanent marker on the lid. When his dad's sister Pearlie Joe had passed away several years before his dad, he had picked up her belongings from the apartment she had shared with a friend. He had given most of her things to charity, but this must have been her personal papers that were of some importance. He had finally reached for the last one and lifting it to set it aside, the bottom fell out of it spilling the contents across the floor. Great, now he had a mess to clean up. He bent down and started picking up the scattered papers and noticed some of them were related to the children's asylum. He guessed they were from her time as a nurse. There was also a stack of pictures with notes attached by paperclips in a small box. Why she had these, and why they were not left in the patient's charts were a mystery. He looked through the pictures and they were enough to make a grown man cry. These poor kids. What they must have went through in their short lives, for most of them never made it out of the hospital. Among those pictures, at the bottom of the pile, was a small framed picture. It was the exact picture he had seen at the asylum when he found the papers strewn about at the nurse station the other day. It was the picture of the nurses and doctors standing out in front of the monstrosity of a building. That must have been why it had seemed familiar to him when he saw it that day. He had to have seen it at his aunt's when he was a kid.

There were several pictures of one boy. Among them was one of him sitting in a swing all alone. You could see other kids in the background playing, but apparently, he was either a loner or the other kids wouldn't play with him. Why did she have so many of this particular boy? He seemed so familiar, there was something about his eyes. All the other pictures had notes attached, these did not. After staring at it for a few moments, Dagan shrugged his shoulders and set them aside.

There were several nursing books as well as books on childhood behavior. He stacked those neatly on top of the boxes he had already moved and placed the pictures back in their small box beside them. He could lose focus on the task at hand, there was so much to look through. It made him wonder about the other boxes that belonged to his aunt.

Now, with those out of the way, he reached for the first box of Rachel's belongings. He noticed something lying on the floor up against it. Reaching down between two boxes, he pulled out what looked like a leather-bound journal. The cover was very worn with age and there was a thin leather strap that wrapped around a small circular piece of leather on the cover keeping it closed. He unwound the strap and flipped through the first few pages. It looked like more notes his aunt had kept. It must have fallen unseen out of the broken box. He laid it with the others and went back to the plastic container. He spent another fifteen minutes sifting through the boxes before finding the yearbooks he had come here for. Rachel was a junior when she disappeared so there were only three. Her freshman and sophomore books were filled with the cute little paragraphs and signatures that kids wrote on yearbook signing day. Her junior yearbook was sadly missing these pledges and promises of staying friends forever no matter where life might take them after graduation. The principal had brought it by the house one day near the end of the school year. It had been a shock to his mom because she had forgotten that Rachel had preordered it at the beginning of the school year.

He found a small empty box and placed the yearbooks in it, then started out of the attic. When he passed by the boxed of his aunt's things, something nagged him about what he had seen earlier. Was it because his current case involved the place she used to work, or the fact she had those pictures and notes?

Out of instinct, he added the pictures, notes and journal to his box with the yearbooks. The weekend had been forecasted to be a rainy one. It would give him plenty of time to read through everything, and maybe give him an idea on which direction to take his investigation.

On his way out, he dialed the sheriff's cell phone. She answered and he asked if she had heard anything back from the lab on the bracelet that had been found with the remains.

"No, nothing yet. I'll call you when I do."

"I appreciate it."

"Where are you? We seem to keep missing each other at the office."

"I stopped by moms. I went through some old yearbooks of Rachel's. I thought since she had a bracelet identical to this one, maybe one of her classmates could be our Jane Doe."

"Good thinking. That's why I keep you on the payroll," she teased.

"I found some things on the asylum too. I don't know if you remember my dad' sister Pearlie Joe. She worked out there and for whatever her reasons, she kept a journal and had things regarding some of the patients. I'm going to look through them when I have a chance. You never know what might turn up. It's just odd we found the remains there, and now I find these things that belonged to her that pertain to the same place."

"I ... I remember her vaguely. What kind of things did she have?"

"Pictures and looks like some type of old medical records. I don't think any of it's relevant, but I happened to come across it and thought it was interesting."

"Sure. Ok. Let me know if you find anything."

"I'll keep you informed." They both hung up and Dagan got an odd feeling from the conversation with her. She had been teasing one minute, then seemed distracted the next.

He had a few hours of work cut out for him with those yearbooks, but whatever he had to do to solve this and possibly find his sister, he was ready for.

CHAPTER II

The rain began early Friday afternoon and did not slack up even a little. By the time Dagan left work, it had already put down three inches. He was thankful he wasn't on call this weekend. The rain always seemed to bring the crazies out.

He knew he would have to hurry home because a lot of times, the dirt roads and bridges would wash out leaving the residents in their rural homes with no accessible way to town until the county came in to make the necessary repairs.

He called ahead to Carol's Café and ordered a cheeseburger with onion rings. He stopped long enough to pick up his order before heading straight home. There was a small creek than ran parallel to the unpaved road to his house, and it had already crested over the top so he knew it would be gone in another hour.

The overcast sky cast an eerie glow in the twilight. When he arrived home, he let the dogs out, but neither stayed out long sensing the dreary weather, nor were they fond of wet grass. They barely made it back in when the angry sky let loose another deluge. He poured food in their bowl and then sat down at the kitchen table to eat. It felt good to relax a little and he was glad to have the weekend off. It had been over a month since he hadn't been on weekend duty.

After finishing off the last onion ring, he threw his plastic containers in the trash and went to the living room only to return a few moments later with the box of things he had brought home from his moms. He had just spread it out on the table when his doorbell rang. Who in the world would be out in this weather? The dogs trotted along behind him eager to see who the visitor might be.

He opened the front door to find his ex-wife standing there drenched to the bone, despite the fact she was holding an umbrella. The rain was blowing sideways so it was doing her little good. He grabbed her by the arm after staring at her momentarily stunned and pulled her into the house.

"Dani, what in the world are you doing out here?"

"Umm, you think I could get a towel, I'm dripping all over your floor, not to mention I'm freezing?" she asked. Kojak and Columbo were excited to see her and Dagan had to tell them to go sit before they knocked her over. This made her giggle and she promised both boys she would give them hugs as soon as she dried off. They immediately went to the edge of the living room carpet and sat.

Dagan quickly went to the bathroom and grabbed two large towels. Dani wrapped one around her shoulders and used the other to dry her dark strawberry blonde hair. She slipped her sneakers off and left them in the foyer. She took one of the towels and threw it on the floor to soak up the puddles she had made.

"I'm sorry to just show up like this. I hope I'm not interrupting anything."

"No, you're not. You are always welcome here, this is still half your house too you know."

Their eyes met briefly and she spoke breaking the spell. "I had a book to deliver to old Mrs. Brantley. She had ordered it a few days ago, and I told her I would bring it to her when it came in since she can't get around right now because of a sprained ankle. When I turned around to head back into town, the road was washed out at Pelham Creek Bridge."

"Like I said, you're more than welcome to stay here. I think there are still some of your clothes in the guest room closet, if you want to change out of those. I can throw them in the washer for you."

"I hope they still fit. I've gained a few pounds."

"You look great. You always have."

"Thanks. I'll just go have a look and see what I can find," she said shyly, scooting around him to go down the hall.

He heard the door to the guest room close so he walked back into the kitchen. This little visit was certainly unexpected. It was several minutes before Dani appeared in the kitchen wearing a pair of sweat pants and long-sleeved t-shirt. Her damp hair had been brushed out. She walked over to Kojak and Columbo where they lay near their food bowls and hugged them both, then patted them on their heads. They greedily accepted her love. "I miss you boys." She whispered to them. Dagan pretended not to notice, but it made him smile. He had made a pot of coffee while she was changing to help warm her. When it had finished brewing he poured two steaming mugs and handed one to her. They both liked it black, no fancy creamers or sugar for them.

"I swear, you still make the best coffee around," she praised after taking a big gulp.

Dagan smiled and replied, "It's the only thing I can cook."

Looking at the table she asked, "Looks like you're working. Are you sure I'm not disturbing you?"

"Dani, you're fine. Really. We had remains turn up the other day at the old children's asylum. I'm trying to put some pieces together to try and figure out who it is."

"I heard about that," she said glancing away. He could tell what she was thinking.

"I've already checked. It's not Rachel."

"I'm sorry. I know what it means to you and your mom to find her."

"Me too. Then again, I'm relieved it wasn't her. It's ridiculous to be both at once."

"Emotions are funny things, and never predictable," Dani said quietly.

"So, what have you been up to?" Dagan said to change the subject.

"Nothing new. The bookstore is doing well. Better than I thought it would."

"That's great! I know it was always your dream to own it. I'm happy to see you happy."

"Are you doing ok? I mean really ... ok?"

"Most of the time. I have days when everything feels like a shit storm, but that's life I guess."

She sat back in her chair and crossed her arms over her chest studying him. He knew that look well. She was trying to figure out what was going on in his head. Dagan wanted to change the subject again. These conversations had led to a lot of arguments and eventually to a divorce.

"So, what did you say happened to Mrs. Brantley?"

"She sprained her ankle walking through the woods. Tripped over a branch or something, fortunately her niece was with her and called the ambulance for help."

"Poor thing."

"Poor thing my foot. She relished the attention, and if rumors are right she was flirting shamelessly with the volunteer firefighters that came to her rescue." She said laughing.

Dagan loved the sound of her laughter. It was like the soft tinkling of a piano. "Wait until I see those guys. I'll have to ask them about how to pick up older women." They were both laughing now. Nostalgia set in for them both. The good times and laughter, right here at this table.

"Nice way to change the subject by the way," Dani chided.

"Well, you know me, always trying to lighten the mood."

"I heard about you and Tracy. I'm sorry it didn't work out for you two."

"It wasn't serious. She wanted more than I was willing to give, that's all."

"Still, I'm sorry."

"Thanks, but I'll survive. I'm surprised nobody has scooped you up. I was a fool and lost you, but surely someone has to be smarter than me."

"I'm surprised you haven't heard."

"Heard what?" he asked with a lump in his throat. Did he really want to know she was seeing someone else?

"Wade has been trying his best to get me to go out with him."

Instant anger filled his gut. He knew Wade would never give up trying, and he had heard some talk around the office, but he wanted to hear her version.

"I thought for sure he would be bragging about it. He has been annoying, but more so lately. He must come by two to three times a week. I'm running out of excuses to turn him down. I thought if I told him I'd think about it, he would back off some," she said clearly agitated.

"Do you want me to say something?"

"No. It would probably make it worse. I can handle him. He's been doing this since high school. Remember?"

"Remember? I have to work with that horse's ass on a daily basis. To top it all off, the sheriff put us both on this latest case."

"What in the world was she thinking?" Dani asked making a face.

"I figure she has either lost her mind or has a sick sense of humor," he responded grinning.

Dani's stomach rumbled loudly at that moment causing them both to laugh. Her cheeks turned pink and she said, "Sorry. I haven't had any supper."

"I have, but I have some things in the fridge. There's sliced deli meat, I can make you a sandwich or an omelet. I remember you used to love those."

"I still love them, but a sandwich is fine and I can make it."

While Dani was putting together her sandwich, Dagan made them both another cup of coffee. They sat back down at the table so Dani could eat.

Kojak and Columbo eyed her cautiously in case she dropped any crumbs on the floor. They knew better than to beg, but dropped food was fair game.

The rain had not slowed down any. As a matter of fact, it was coming down harder, if that was possible. A bolt of lightning split the sky briefly illuminating the darkness accompanied by a loud clap of thunder. It caused Dani to jump, and both dogs perked their ears up.

"Dang, that was loud, and close by," she said grabbing her chest with one hand.

"It sure was. I'm surprised we still have power. Normally my electricity goes out with just barely a sprinkle and a light breeze." He walked over and looked out the window. "I don't think you're going anywhere anytime soon. If that road wasn't washed completely out earlier, it is now."

"I was hoping you'd let me stay here. It was that, or sleep in my car, or stay with Mrs. Brantley. Frankly, I would take my car over her. She never shuts up," she said stuffing the last bite of sandwich in her mouth.

"You're not sleeping in your car. You can have my bed and I'll take the couch."

"I noticed you got rid of the bed in the guest room."

"Yeah, a guy at work needed a bed for his kids so I let him have it."

"Ok, but I can sleep on the couch. I don't want to put you out of your bed."

"No arguments. You can have the bedroom. Of course, you may have two men in there with you. I hope you don't mind snoring." He said pointing to the canine pair.

"Oh God, two men snoring? What did I ever do?" she said throwing her head back in exaggerated aggravation.

"I'm sure there's something in your past you're paying for," he teased. He loved to watch her smile at the good-natured ribbing.

"Seriously, thanks."

"It's no problem at all."

"I wanted to take a shower, but with this lightening I think it's best to wait until morning."

"No kidding. It's popping all over out there." Just as Dagan said this, the lights went out. "I knew it was bound to happen sooner or later. Let me get some lanterns out of the hall closet. He made his way slowly in the darkness, being careful not to bump into anything down the hallway and to the closet. He grabbed three battery-powered lanterns that he kept there with extra batteries just for this very thing. It was a common occurrence to lose power in a rainstorm in this neck of the woods. He placed one on the counter, one on the table and the other on a small table between the kitchen and living room. A bright flash of lightning lit the entire sky for a few seconds.

"What was that?" Dani stood and walked towards the window.

"What was what?" Dagan asked following her.

"I could have sworn I saw something or someone outside just now when the lightning flashed."

They both stood trying to peer out into the darkness. She pointed in the direction of the driveway. "Right there, near the mailbox."

"If there is someone out there, they are nuts." He looked some more trying to see what was out there. "I don't see anyone. Maybe the light was playing tricks on your eyes."

"Maybe, but it sure looked like someone."

They both looked a few more seconds and then returned to the table.

"How about we take all this stuff in the living room. We can sit in there where it's more comfortable and look through this stuff. Maybe you can help solve a mystery." He said scooping up everything and throwing it all in the box. Dani carried the lanterns, leaving one in the kitchen but turning it off, and followed Dagan into the living room. Dagan started a fire in the fireplace. Although it was late March, the temperatures could still be cold here at night, especially after a long rain. Besides that, it gave them added light to read by.

Dagan dug through the yearbooks and chose Rachel's freshman year. He thumbed through to her class and began looking over the names of her classmates. Some he recognized because they were younger siblings to his own classmates. Others he recognized from them hanging out with his little sister. There were, of course, others he didn't know at all. These were going to be his focus. He got a notepad and pen from the desk in the corner of the living room and handed it to Dani.

"Would you mind writing names down as I call them out? Your handwriting is so much neater than mine."

"Sure, whatever I can do to help."

He began calling out the names of the kids he didn't know. He was certain none of the names he recognized were missing persons. He got the sophomore book next and did the same, then last, her junior yearbook.

"Can you tell me what you're thinking with these names?" Dani asked looking over the list.

"I don't recognize any of them. I'm certain that none of Rachel's friends, whose names I know, went missing around the same time she did. There are other names that are familiar because they had older siblings that we went to school with. None of them are missing as far as I know. I'm going to compare the unknown names to the ones I have from the FCIC database of missing people that I have case files on."

"What can I do to help?"

"You can go through these lists and if a name appears on all three lists, mark it with a yellow highlighter." He handed her a highlighter and she got started. He got up and walked around to the back of couch. He had placed his leather pouch there that he carried work home in. He found the missing persons files, and took the list from the top of it that he had made earlier that week. He placed it all on the coffee table and asked Dani if she would like anything from the kitchen. She asked him for a bottle of water so he walked to the refrigerator to grab them both a bottle. He also picked up a plastic container of cookies his mom had given him to bring home the other night. They were his favorite, white chocolate macadamia nut. He returned to the living room and asked, "Did you find anything interesting yet?"

"Actually, I did. Almost all the names were on these three lists except for these. There is a Nikki Butler, Charles Dart, Anita Harris, Bobby White, and Tammy White. The last two names are on the junior list, but not the freshman or sophomore lists. Nikki Butler, Charles Dart, and Anita Harris are on the sophomore and junior lists. None of them are on the freshman list."

"They must have transferred in from other schools, or moved here from another place. At least I have a starting point. Since the remains we found were female, I guess we can mark off all the male names except Bobby White. He might have info on Tammy White if they are related."

"I think I'm calling it a night detective. I would love to help out some more, but I can barely hold my eyes open thanks to the warm fire."

He glanced up and smiled. "You never could stay up past 10:00."

"Some things never change. I need my beauty sleep."

"Thanks for your help."

"You're welcome. Maybe if I ever retire from selling books, I'll start a new career." She stood and walked down the hall to the bedroom. He watched her until she disappeared through the doorway.

He realized now just how much he missed her. He was finally able to admit it to himself, but could he ever admit it to her?

CHAPTER 12

Dani lay in the bed and watched the lightening dance across the ceiling periodically. She hadn't lied to Dagan about being sleepy, she was exhausted. Being here in this room where they had shared so many loving moments. She found herself restless. She wasn't sure what strange twist of fate had brought her here this evening, but she was glad for it.

It had felt warm and familiar.

It had felt right.

She missed those feelings of comfort when she and Dagan had been married. He made her feel safe, and she realized now she missed him more than she ever thought possible after two years of being divorced. She had come to the realization a long time ago that she had jumped the gun and should have never filed for a divorce. All marriages have their problems and rough spots, and she should have seen them through instead of running away. She had never been good at handling personal issues, and Dagan had plenty stemming from his missing sister, to the death of his father who had been his hero.

She should have been more patient and helped him, instead of resenting the time he had spent looking for his sister.

She had been ready to ask forgiveness, and a second chance, when she learned that Dagan was dating someone else. That had lasted about a year, and Dani had started to think that Dagan was gone for good, when she heard that he was no longer seeing anyone. Maybe this was her second chance.

Even though the quilt on the bed was heavy, the damp cold seeped into the room causing her to shiver.

Without power, there was no way to heat the room. She grabbed her pillow and blanket and walked down the hall. She could see the reflection of the fire on the walls and walked back into the room, surprising Dagan.

"Couldn't sleep?"

"It's too cold in there. Mind if I crash out here by the fire?"

"Go ahead. Take the couch. I'll sleep in the recliner."

"First, I took your bed, now I'm taking the couch. I'm an awful house guest."

"I told you earlier, this is still your house too. Always will be. It didn't change after the divorce and it never will." He never looked up from his paperwork.

"Still, I feel guilty."

"If you feel guilty, tomorrow I'll let you do dishes and mop the floors. How's that?"

"I might not feel that guilty."

This time he looked up and grinned. "That's what I thought."

She remained quiet and just watched him as he shuffled through papers and took notes. He rubbed his eyes every now and then and she knew he was tired too. Dagan always worked too hard. She realized now it was just part of who he was, and loved him for it. As if he sensed her watching him, he looked up. She blushed but knew it would be hard to tell in the firelight of the room. It gave everything a pinkish orange glow.

They both started to say something at the same time, and then laughed nervously.

"You go first." He said.

"I'm not sure if what I'm about to say is what you want to hear."

"Try me, nothing is worse than hearing you say you wanted a divorce."

72

That stung, even though she was sure he hadn't meant it to. Her eyes brimmed with tears. "I'm so sorry Dagan. I should have never..." She couldn't finish her statement.

In the blink of an eye, he was beside her on the couch with his arms around her. She was almost sobbing now. She didn't deserve his kindness, and it was in that moment that she knew he still loved her too.

"Stop. We both made mistakes and neither of us can take the sole responsibility for the end of the marriage."

She couldn't bear to look at him. She had caused him a lot of pain in addition to what he had already suffered. He should hate her.

"I still love you Dagan." She mustered up the bravado from down deep to barely whisper those few words. He remained silent for a few minutes. His chin was resting on the top of her head so she couldn't tell by his facial expression what he might be thinking. He placed his hand under her chin and turned her face up to look at him.

"I love you too. I've never stopped."

"Do you want to try and work it out? Being here tonight has really made me want to come home and made me realize that I should have never left."

"I want you back home too. It's all I've ever wanted, but I loved you enough to let you go if that's what it took for you to be happy."

"I want to take things slow. I want to make sure we get it right this time because I never want to be this miserable again like the past two years has been."

"I agree, whatever it takes."

She reached up and kissed him softly, and then laid her head against his chest. The soft beat of his heart sounded like a distant drum and lulled her into deep settled state. Within minutes she was sound asleep. Feeling content, Dagan soon followed.

~ ~ ~

Kojak and Columbo were peacefully aware that their master and mistress were sound asleep. They were also aware of sounds coming from outside the house. The rain and howling wind were fierce, but these sounds were different.

These were footsteps, and they sounded as if they were getting closer and heavier. Kojak was the first to perk his ears up and notice that the footsteps were on the porch. Although he never lifted his head, he kept his partially closed eyes on the window in the living room. The curtains were partially open and there was a gap of about 6 inches, allowing him to see outside. The noise seemed to be gone so he closed his eyes again.

Suddenly, Columbo began with a low growl in his throat causing Kojak to spring his eyes open. He looked at the opening in the window, only now there was a black shadow covering it. He jumped to his feet and began barking, causing his brother to bark also.

This startled Dagan and Dani awake. Dagan looked around disoriented and saw the dogs barking at the front window. When he glanced up, he saw the outline of a shadow too, but suddenly it was gone.

He quickly disentangled himself from Dani and ran towards the window. He opened a drawer in the small table in the foyer and grabbed a pistol. He carefully opened the front door and looked around. There was nobody there.

"Lock this door behind me." He instructed Dani, and he stepped out on the porch. Rain and wind slashed his skin. It felt like tiny ice needles. He walked the entire perimeter of the house on the wraparound porch. There was no one around, and he couldn't see far enough in the darkness to tell if anyone was out there in the woods. He returned to the front door to see Dani's worried face looking out the window. She hurriedly opened the door and handed him the blanket they had been sleeping under.

"Did you find anyone?"

"No, but now I'm thinking you might have seem someone earlier."

"Why would anybody be sneaking around here?"

"I have no idea. Probably a couple of kids looking to steal something. I have the ATVs in the barn out back. I keep all my fishing equipment out there too. A lot of that stuff gets stolen all the time. I used to take reports on it weekly."

"It gives me the creeps that someone night have been out there watching us through the window."

Dagan quickly pulled the curtains closed.

"Try to go back to sleep. I'll look around in the morning when there's some light to work with."

Dani settled back down on the couch and was back asleep in minutes. Dagan on the other hand was wide awake and worried. He had never had any trouble with trespassers or thieves out here. The neighbors he had were all older, and none had any younger relatives living with them to his knowledge.

Why would anybody be out in this type of weather for any reason other than work? He was afraid there was far more to it than he had told Dani. He hadn't wanted to worry her, but he himself was concerned. Who could be snooping around his place, and what could they possibly be looking for?

CHAPTER 13

By morning, the heavy rains had subsided to only a slow and steady drizzle. According to the weather report though, it would return later today.

Dagan never fell back asleep last night after the dogs had woke them up. His mind had been too busy running scenarios of who could have been outside, and why they were here. His imagination had taken from the simple possibility of a thief, as he had told Dani, through the worst possibility of someone he had once put away coming after him for revenge.

The electricity has come back on in the early morning hours but it had been spotty. It would come on and then flicker.

Dani and the dogs were still sleeping. He left her on the couch and pulled a blanket up over her shoulders. He threw another log on the fire and stoked it to get it going again then walked over to the front door. He pulled a rain coat off the peg on the wall and pulled on his mud boots.

He stepped out into a cool still morning. A blanket of fog hung around the edges of his yard in the wooded area of his property, giving the forest a fairy tale ambience. Stepping off the porch, he walked out to the mailbox. That is where Dani had said she saw someone last night. He looked around for footprints but knew it was futile. The rain would have washed away any that had been there however briefly last night. He returned to the porch and looked at the window where he had seen the peeping tom. There was mud, but no discernable prints. At least he knew he hadn't being seeing things, even though the dogs' reactions were really the only proof he needed.

After checking the rest of the yard, and then checking his barn to see if anything had been stolen, he went back in the house. Dani and the dogs were still asleep, so he headed to the kitchen to put some coffee on and make breakfast. He took eggs and bacon from the refrigerator and set them on the counter. He got a loaf of bread from the top of the refrigerator, where he had to keep it to keep the dogs from getting it off the counter and eating it when they were feeling mischievous.

Once he got the bacon going in the oven, he put on a pot of coffee. While he was whisking the eggs, Dani came into the kitchen rubbing her eyes.

"Morning..." she mumbled.

"Good morning. Have a seat. Breakfast will be ready in a few minutes."

"It smells good, so does the coffee."

"One cup coming right up." Dagan walked over and set the steaming mug of joe in front of her, and then kissed the top of her head. She watched him as he worked. She liked seeing him being so domestic. He never had the time or the inclination when they had been married, but she guessed being single he had to do it. She thought he looked cute with a dishtowel slung over his shoulders making sure that his eggs weren't burning. The toast popped up just as he was scooping the eggs out of the pan and putting them on the plates. He added the slices of toast to each plate, and then a few pieces of bacon he had just taken from the oven. He walked over and put the plates down.

"Ummm, it looks delicious." Dani complimented.

"Oh, I forgot the butter and jelly for the toast." Dagan went to the refrigerator to grab them. They both prepared their toast and then dug in. They mostly ate in silence but it wasn't an uncomfortable silence. It was one of familiarity and contentment.

"I guess you've been practicing your cooking skills." Dani said breaking the quiet.

"I think you're just hungry! Besides, it's hard to screw up bacon, eggs and toast."

"I guarantee I could do it. Anyway, I'm enjoying it."

"What are you planning to do today?"

"Well, I can't get back to town so I guess you're stuck with me for at least another day or so."

"No other way I'd rather be stuck." He grinned. Why was it his devilish smile could still make her blush after all these years?

"What did you have planned for the weekend before me and the rain came along?"

"Working on the same stuff I worked on last night."

"If you don't need my expertise. I am going to go through the things I left here. If I haven't needed it in two years, I probably don't need it at all."

"True, but some of those things are pictures and stuff like that. There are also some things you saved from high school, and some of your family's albums."

"Sounds like enough to keep me occupied while you work."

They finished up and rinsed their dishes and placed them in the dishwasher. Dagan let the dogs out for a bathroom break and Dani headed off to the back bedroom. When the dogs had finished, Dagan settled in the living room where he would be more comfortable. After getting everything situated, curiosity got the best of him and he grabbed the old records from the asylum.

He hesitated for a moment thinking he was wasting time on this when he should be trying to put the puzzle pieces, what few he had, together to figure out who the remains found belonged to. Something was nagging at him to look through the records, and his gut instinct had never failed him.

The paperwork before him read like a lot of medical documents with terminology he wasn't familiar with or could even begin to understand. His aunts' side notes, however, were a different story.

Her jottings were mostly of treatments that the children received. Some of them were so barbaric, it seemed as if he was reading pages from a bad horror novel. He was more inclined to think these so-called treatments were not given, so much as perpetrated upon these kids.

Electroshock therapy, lobotomies, ice baths, physical restraints, and isolation were the most common. Many physical and mental illnesses, it seemed, were thought to be one in the same.

He read that some patients were given doses of the drug Metrazol to chemically induce seizures to cure whatever mental illness the patient has been diagnosed with. High doses of insulin could also be prescribed and was called insulin shock therapy. The latter was primarily used to treat schizophrenia.

Dagan could not believe that his aunt would have had a part in this. She had always been so loving and kind to him and Rachel. He had heard his parents talk about her huge heart for children, and what a shame it was she had never had any of her own. How could she have witnessed this cruelty and not spoken up or alerted the authorities? He knew times were different then, but surely, she could have got someone to listen.

He moved on to the pictures and found those just as disturbing. A small boy about eight or nine years old sat on the concrete floor. He had been placed in a strait jacket and then tied to a radiator in the room. The light from the window above the radiator reflected off the tears streaming down his face, and there was utter despair in his eyes. A lump had formed in the back of Dagan's throat, and he found it hard to stop looking into the boy's eyes. There was literally nothing this child could have done to warrant this kind of treatment, especially at his age. Dagan wished he could reach through the photograph and save the boy, to release him from his torture.

The next picture was not any better. A young girl was sitting on a wooden chair that resembled a training potty, only this was adult size. Her arms were strapped down to the arms of the chair and there was a metal helmet-like apparatus on her head that had a cage made of screen. What was the purpose of this? Was it to keep her from biting someone? He hoped she had bit whoever put her in the contraption and it had hurt like hell.

He shuffled through the stack of pictures that had naked children sitting on the floor with their knees drawn up to their chests, countless kids so rail thin he wasn't sure they could had even stood up on their own power, much less walked. Near the bottom of the stack, he came across pictures of the boy that had seemed familiar to him the other day.

As hard as he tried, he could not make the connection, but he was sure he knew the kid from somewhere. It was more than a feeling, it was a strange sort of vibe.

Dani came out of the back room asking him about trash bags.

"Come over here a minute." He requested. She walked over and he handed her the pictures.

"Does he seem familiar to you?"

She studied the pictures for a few moments and said, "You know, he does a little bit."

"Who could he be I wonder?"

"I'm not sure." She pointed to the picture and traced his face with her finger, "right here around the eyes."

Dagan looked and responded, "I thought the same thing."

Dani shrugged her shoulders. "Maybe it'll come to one of us sooner or later." She handed the picture back to Dagan and asked, "Are the garbage bags still under the kitchen sink?"

He answered yes, but never looked up from the picture. After a few seconds, he set it aside, and reached for the leather journal. He had barely glanced through it the other day, but now settled himself on the couch and propped his feet up so he could read comfortably. He could hear just the slightest sound of rain on the roof. A drizzle had begun that would lead to heavier rains again tonight.

He unwound the leather strap from around its hold and opened it up, careful with the pages, as some of them were sticking together. The pages were yellowed from age and some of the ink was faded in some spots, but still legible. The handwriting was precise and neat.

The first few pages had him realizing what he should have known earlier. His aunt had been collecting information to use as evidence to convince someone to help these children. He should've known she could never be a part of such sinister cruelty and neglect. She had notes on different children and even wrote down things the nurses had said to the children.

Cruel things, no child should ever hear.

He was so engrossed in the journal, he hadn't noticed that Dani walked through several times. She finally commented on her latest pass through that she was getting hungry causing him to look at his wristwatch and saw it was 11:30. It was almost lunch time, and he hadn't even noticed the passing of time.

He called out asking her if she would like a grilled ham and cheese and she said she did. He went to the kitchen and the dogs followed him. They knew it was time to eat too. He filled their bowls with kibble and they greedily ate it. He gathered the things he would need to make the sandwiches and had them ready in less than ten minutes. Dani joined him and poured them both a glass of tea and set them on the table with plates and napkins. When Dagan was done, he carried the frying pan over to the table and used the spatula to put a sandwich on each plate.

"Sorry I didn't notice what time it was. It seems my Aunt Pearlie Joe's journal is hard to put down."

"Good stuff huh?"

"More like sad stuff. The kids in that asylum went through pure hell."

"I remember hearing stories about that place when we were kids. My mom and grandma knew someone that had their child placed there. They always tried to talk in hushed voices so me and my sisters wouldn't hear, but we did. It scared us so bad sometimes, we would be really good for the next week or so after listening to the stories. We were scared if we were bad, we would have to go there for punishment."

"These kids were the ones that society rejected for things such as Downs syndrome, epilepsy and ADHD. Then there were some that were put away for simple things like bedwetting. It's heartbreaking, but people didn't have the medical knowledge about those things that we do today. If they had, those kid's lives might have been a lot different."

"I suppose. They were all victims of the times and parents who expected perfection. It's hard for me to wrap my head around putting any kid of mine away just because they had a medical condition." Dani said shaking her head.

They both finished their sandwiches thinking about those poor kids. Finally, Dagan broke the silence by asking, "Did you manage to weed out the good stuff you want to keep?"

"Did you not see me walk through the living room with four bags of trash?" she asked while pointing to the place where she stacked them by the back door.

Turning to look he replied sheepishly, "Yeah well, like I said, the journal is pretty interesting reading."

She rolled her eyes and exhaled a big "Uh huh."

"Let's both take a break. I know it's drizzling outside, but I have some rain coats. You want to take a walk in the woods? The dogs could use the exercise." he asked.

"Sounds fun. Let me pull my hair up and put on my sneakers." She stood to leave the table, but he grabbed her by the wrist and pulled her down into his lap.

"I know you want to take things slow, but exactly how slow are we talking?" he needed to know so he wouldn't push her too far.

"Dagan, I'm not even sure I know what I meant, so it would be hard to explain it to you. All I can say is that if I feel we're moving too fast, I'll let you know."

He kissed her softly on the lips and she didn't resist. "Is that ok?" he asked resting his forehead on hers.

"That's definitely ok." She whispered. They shared another kiss, this time it lasted a little longer.

"It's hard being this close to you and not taking it any further" he murmured.

"It's hard for me too, but I was serious Dagan. Please, let's take our time."

"I think we should take that walk now before I get smacked for doing things you may not be ready for."

"I would never smack you ... not hard anyway," she said smiling. She stood and walked out of the kitchen leaving him to clean the mess. That was perfectly fine with him though, he needed to cool down. He had forgotten how much he loved her kisses, but he hadn't forgotten how much he loved her, and he never would.

~ ~ ~

The woods were cool and quiet. The air had a crisp quality made even more so by the light sprinkling of rain, but the wind had died down to just a slight breeze. Dani and Dagan walked along hand in hand while Kojak and Columbo roamed ahead of them, sniffing every tree and bush, and marking a few every now and then. Dani made some joke about the dogs being dehydrated by the time they made it back home if they didn't stop peeing on everything and Dagan laughed easily. He felt the happiest he had felt in a long time. Everything seemed normal for once. He was amazed. A couple of weeks ago, he had a girlfriend walk out of their relationship that he wasn't happy with anyway, and now a rainstorm had brought Dani back into his life.

Dani found a stick on the ground and threw it for the dogs. She laughed at the way they both picked up one end of it and started playing tug-o-war with it. She ran to catch up with them leaving Dagan behind to watch all three of them, and laugh at his boys and his wife, his ex-wife, whatever. Watching his steps through a washed-out part of the path, he noticed bushes that looked as if they had been trampled down. He looked closer and noticed some tire tracks that looked like they could have come from an ATV. Someone had been out here on his property. Were there poachers coming onto his land hoping to bag a buck or hog? They had caught some down the road on the Harvey's place not long ago. Mrs. Harvey dang near got shot while hanging out her sheets on the clothesline from a stray bullet.

Was that who had been wandering around last night? He hadn't heard anything that had sounded like an ATV, but the rain and wind would have covered the noise.

He would keep a closer watch tonight. Something was going on out here. He didn't like to think someone unknown to him was wondering around on his property doing god knows what.

From this spot, he had a clear view of his back porch. Someone could easily watch the house from here.

Dani was still playing fetch with the dogs oblivious to what he was looking at. He wanted to keep it that way. There was no need to worry her.

Dani had not even noticed how ever so often Kojak would stop and look around, sniffing the wind, but Dagan did. Playing was more important at the moment though, so he continued to chase sticks, and play tug of war with Dani and Columbo, content to let his master do all the worrying.

CHAPTER 14

ani and Dagan returned about an hour later wet from the rain, but content. They hung their raincoats up on a peg by the back door and Dagan threw an old towel on the floor so they would not drip all over.

The dogs stood on the back porch and shook. After they were satisfied with their semi dry coats, they went to lay on the spot in front of the fireplace. They both had a blanket that Dagan had put down for them last night to sleep on and it seemed to be the perfect place for a nap.

Dagan suggested grilling steaks for supper. He had bought a couple the other day and put them in the fridge. One had been for the boys, but they would have to give it up for Dani. What they didn't know wouldn't hurt them. Dagan kept his grill on the back porch so the rain wouldn't be a problem if the wind stayed calm and not blowing like it was last night. He would season them with herbs and spices then place them back in the fridge. He searched the refrigerator and found some ears of corn and broccoli that would go perfect with the steaks later. With his meal planned out, all he had to do now was to season the steaks. He would finish up in here, then join Dani in the living room to watch a movie.

~ ~ ~

Dani had left Dagan in the kitchen to prepare the steaks for later. He had become pretty good at cooking since the divorce. She guessed he did what he had to do. She on the other hand, would rather order pizza or eat a sandwich than cook. Settling on the couch, she picked up the journal that Dagan had been so into earlier. She took her thumb and flipped the pages quickly and noticed something out of place towards the back. She thumbed the pages again but slowly this time, until she found the spot that was seemed different. She found a small wallet sized picture and what looked to be two letters that had been folded in half. She studied the picture and saw that it was the same little boy that she and Dagan had thought looked familiar earlier. The letters seemed stuck in between the pages. She pulled on them carefully so as not to damage either the book or the letters. They eventually came out with a little patience.

She carefully unfolded the first one and started reading. Her eyes widened in disbelief. She quickly unfolded the second letter and was shocked even further.

"Dagan?" she called out.

"Yeah."

"You better come look at this."

"Give me a sec." He walked into the room wiping his hands on a kitchen towel. "What?"

Without a word, she handed the picture and letters to him. He could see the picture was the same one before that looked familiar. Flipping the picture over, the letters WJB were written in faded black ink. Were these his initials? It took him a couple of minutes to examine the letters, then he quietly mouthed, "What the hell?"

"That's what I was thinking." They simply looked at each other stunned.

"How could this be? I've never heard anything about this," Dagan responded incredulously.

"You would know better than I would. It's your family," she responded.

"In all these years, how did I never know that she had a baby? She never mentioned it. Hell, nobody has ever mentioned it."

"Are you going to ask around?"

"I'm not sure yet. I mean you don't just walk up to someone and say so when were you going to tell me you had a baby who apparently is no longer a part of your life. I mean, what happened to him? Is he alive? Did she place him up for adoption? Did she have him put in the asylum for some reason, or did someone else? There are so many questions!"

"You think your parents knew about this?"

"If they did they never said anything. I mean Alice is my boss and my godmother. She's my mother's best friend. You would think in all these years, I would have heard something about it. Apparently, my aunt knew about it so I cannot imagine my mother didn't know."

"Are you going to ask her?"

"This is obviously something Alice didn't want anyone knowing about. Best friends keep secrets, and Mom is her best friend. I think I'll dig around a little before I bring it up. Sometimes secrets are meant to stay buried. Is the kid in the picture the one the letters are talking about? Is that why he seems familiar?"

"What if he turns out to be one of the kids that went missing from that place? Wasn't there some whackadoodle doctor out there doing strange experiments on the kids?"

"I think that was mostly urban legend."

"I'm not sure about that. There were kids that were listed on the hospital census that were nowhere to be found when the state came in to shut them down. They weren't listed as deceased so what happened to them? Some people think they are buried out behind the building in unmarked graves after whatever experiment was being performed on them went wrong."

"Again, that could be just rumor."

"There's always some truth in every story like that. I think there's a history book at the store on the area and there's a chapter on the hospital. I'll look and see what I can find out."

"It's got me wondering now if the remains we found there has a connection to the asylum or if it's just a coincidence it was found there. Do you think I'm making a mountain out of a molehill?"

"I'm not sure. What I do know is that you're brilliant at figuring these things out." She put her arms around his waist and he pulled her in for a hug.

"I'm glad you have confidence in me. I'm not sure I can figure this one out without upsetting a lot of people. I would rather avoid that if I can."

"It may not be possible. Secrets have a way of coming out and they usually don't create a lot of happiness when they do."

He hugged her tighter. He certainly had a lot to think about. There were two things he was certain about. The first was Dani was here right now, and the second was he would never let work get in between them again. He was setting all this aside for a few hours to watch a movie with her. They settled on the couch and snuggled under a light quilt to watch a comedy that they had both seen a dozen times, but it was one of their favorites. About thirty minutes in, he noticed Dani's breathing had evened out and she wasn't giggling anymore. Looking down, he saw she was asleep.

He laughed quietly. Some things never change. She could never make it through an entire movie. Oh well, he laid his head back and closed his eyes. Before long, he had joined her in a nice long afternoon nap.

CHAPTER 15

Knocking on the door brought Dani and Dagan out of their sleep this time instead of barking dogs. Dagan answered to find his neighbor Mr. Harvey standing there.

"Mr. Harvey, what can I do for you?" Dagan motioned for him to come inside out of the rain. He removed his hat and held it with both hands.

"Someone was between our properties last night. I saw somebody out there walking around. I thought it was you at first having no reason to think it was anyone else. Problem is, he was dressed completely in black with one of them sweatshirts the kids call hoodies. I couldn't see his face. When I called out to him, it scared him and he ran off. It was raining too hard for me to go after him. I just made sure my guns were loaded and by my side all night."

"We saw someone last night too. Dani saw him out by the mailbox and later, someone was standing on my front porch looking in my window." He said unconsciously pointing to the window.

"You reckon it was them poachers from awhile back?"

"Could be. Might be some meth head out looking for something to steal. The best thing to do is lock up at night and keep an eye out. You said you have your guns loaded. You should be ok. Let me know if you need anything. Do you have my number?"

"You gave it to the missus last time I had to go out of town for a few days. It's just me and her out there and we are getting on in age. I appreciate your time."

91

"No problem at all." Dagan told him, and then watched him climb into his old green Ford pickup truck that had seen better days and drive away.

"At least we know we weren't the only ones seeing the boogey man last night," Dani said from the couch, after Dagan closed the door.

"Whoever he is, he'd better be careful. I get the feeling that old man doesn't play. He's locked and loaded if the guy comes back around."

"Do you think it's something to really worry about?"

"I'm not sure, but like I told Mr. Harvey, we'll keep an eye out. We have the Bobbsey twins over there that will certainly let us know if anyone comes up."

"They didn't bark just now when your neighbor came calling." She pointed out teasing him.

"That's because they didn't sense any danger from the old man. Look at them, they are vicious guard dogs." They both looked and Kojak was snoring and Columbo was lying on his back with all fours in the air. He too was snoring. They both burst into laughter.

"I certainly feel safer here with you and the troops over there."

"How about we go get the grill started and have an early supper. The rain is starting to get a little harder and I would like to be done in case the power goes out again."

"Sounds good to me."

"Kojak, Columbo, let's go outside." Dagan had no more got the words out of his mouth and they were both awake and running to the back door. They were always ready for an outdoor adventure. They quickly ran to the edge of the yard as soon as he opened the back door, did their business, then returned to the porch. There were a few of their toys in a basket by the door and they helped themselves to a couple to play with.

The steaks were done in no time it seemed as Dagan sipped on a beer and Dani had a glass of wine. The corn and broccoli took even less time, and they enjoyed each other's company over their meal. There were moments it felt as if they hadn't been apart for the past two years. The only problem was, they had been. It was going to take time to get back to where they both wanted to be.

Just as they were finishing up eating, the lights flickered but managed to stay on.

"We better get these dishes done before we lose power again, or they'll have to wait until morning." Dani said.

They made quick work of the cleanup. With that finished, they went to relax on the couch, but Dani decided on a shower instead. She hadn't been able to take one last night due to the lightening and the power being off. The water would have been ice cold since the hot water heater wasn't running with no power.

Dagan walked around the house checking the windows and doors making sure everything was locked up tight. He went to his gun cabinet and took out a Remington 870 12-gauge shotgun, and his service weapon, a Glock .22. Either one would be easy for Dani to handle, should the need arise. Her dad had made sure his girls had the necessary skills to survive, and for life in the country.

He pulled the curtains in the living room and checked the ones in the bedroom and found them already pulled closed. The couch had killed his back last night and this afternoon, so he was going to sleep in the bed tonight. When he had suggested it to Dani after her shower, she eyed him suspiciously making him grin. "To sleep only, scouts honor."

"You were never a boy scout." She chastised teasingly.

They made their way down the hall with Kojak and Columbo following close behind. They too had missed their beds under the picture window.

Once everyone had settled, the house seemed peaceful. The only noise that could be heard was the sound of wind and rain. Dani scooted closer to Dagan. He knew her well and understood she wanted to be held. He knew she was thinking about whoever had been outside last night, and if they would return tonight. He wrapped his arm around her waist and pulled her close, placing his chin atop her head. This was going to be pure torture he thought.

They drifted off to sleep, unaware that someone indeed had returned to find all the curtains were drawn. Anger seethed from the would-be creeper, but this was a problem that could be easily solved. Someone would have to die.

CHAPTER 16

Monday morning dawned bright sunshine. The DOT was out working to get the road passable after nine inches of rainfall.

Dagan called the station and told them he would be in as soon as he could get over the bridge. Nobody was concerned, because that was life in this part of Florida. Pure country, and most of them lived in the same types of rural areas.

Dani, on the other hand, had to call her friend Beth to open the book store for her until she could get there. Of course, she was more than happy to, and wanted to hear all the details of how Dani had come to spend the weekend with her ex-husband.

The road worker Dagan had spoken to told him the road should be open within the next hour so he and Dani had breakfast while they waited.

The same guy stopped by a bit later and let them know the road was accessible. They said their goodbyes and shared a sweet kiss that lasted longer than either had anticipated, got in their vehicles and made the slow progression down the road that had become washboard like from the pounding rains, and over the bridge that was now very narrow from the temporary repair.

Dagan arrived at the station and noticed Alice was not in her office. Her secretary said she was in a meeting down at City Hall and would be back later. He was glad because he was not sure how he would react seeing her right now. Of course, he would not say anything about what he knew, but he hoped he could act normal so she wouldn't suspect anything out of the ordinary. He still was not sure what, if anything, it had to do with his case, but he had the oddest feeling it did.

He heard a desk drawer slam shut and looked up to see Wade bounce a pen off his desk top. He seemed agitated. Dagan had the strong urge to go over and egg it on, whatever it was, but quelled it. He had bigger problems to deal with.

He wanted to call the records department at the county hospital to see if he could find the birth records for the boy in the pictures, but knew he would need a subpoena. That would mean that the sheriff would know what he was trying to do.

Frustration set in because all he had to go on were the initials that had been written on the back of the picture.

WJB

He let out a huge sigh, and let it go for now. He needed to get back to the case at hand. He pulled out the list of names he and Dani had put together. He ran each name through the FCIC. The reports were basic for the first one, a couple of speeding tickets, but not much else for Nikki Butler.

Next up was Anita Harris and apparently, she had been a little too fond of the bottle. She had several DUI's.

That left him with Bobby and Tammy White. Were they related, or was it just that they shared a common last name? The only yearbook either of them had been listed in was Rachel's junior yearbook. Chances were high that they were brother and sister, and had moved here that year.

He ran Bobby's name first. He had a couple of run-ins as a juvenile, but had kept himself clean since then.

He was surprised when he ran Tammy's name and found nothing. She didn't even have a driver's license in the system. That was odd. A young woman in her mid-twenties with no driver's license? He checked for a state I.D. card and found nothing.

Her last known address was 319 Orchard Street. It was the poorest section of town back then, and still was.

Bobby's last known address as listed on his driver's license was 1103 Cross Hill Road.

It looked as if he would be paying a visit to both addresses in hopes of finding answers. He hit the print button for both reports and walked over to grab them off the printer.

Looking over at the Sheriff's office, he still found it empty. Her secretary was over at the coffee pot talking to a dispatcher, so he walked over apologizing for interrupting to let her and dispatch know where he would be.

He noticed Wade was gone as well. He hadn't seen him but briefly this morning, but hadn't noticed him leaving either.

He wished Wade was like any other guy on this force. He would gladly share information and ideas with him. He didn't want to work against him, but Wade's attitude didn't allow a proper partnership. Dagan had really tried to put the past behind him, after all, high school was over fifteen years ago. It was time to be grown-ups and play nice. Every time he gave it an effort, Wade threw up a roadblock by making a snide comment, or brought up something long forgotten, and pissed Dagan off. He imagined it would be that way forever. When Wade finally realized that he and Dani were back together, he really would turn up the BS a couple of notches. There was just no helping it.

He gathered his things and walked out to his patrol truck. He finally got it back from the mechanics shop and was glad. He had been driving his personal vehicle because the only patrol car that had been available had an air conditioner that wasn't working. Just problems of small town departments he thought. He had to have new brakes put on his patrol truck and they had taken their sweet time with it.

Glad to have it back, he headed out to find Tammy White at her last known address.

He arrived on Orchard Street within minutes, and noticed the curious stares from the residents who lived in the neighborhood. His patrol vehicle made him stand out. Every house on the street looked the same except the paint color. They were rundown leftovers from the 1960's. Some were taken care of as best as low income would allow, others looked as if they should be red-tagged for demolition. He found 319, and could see an old man sitting on the front porch in a lawn chair.

He pulled in slowly and turned off the ignition. The old man never said a word as Dagan walked up to the steps of the porch, but pushed his hat up a little further on his head so he could see him better.

"Good afternoon sir. I'm detective Murphy with the Washington County Sheriff's office. I was wondering if Tammy White might still be living here."

"Never heard of her. I've been living here for near 8 years now."

"And your name is?"

"Benson. Jack Benson."

"You didn't know the people who lived here before you?"

"Nope. Bought the house through a realtor. Never knew who the house belonged to before that, although I think I heard it had been a rental."

"You happen to have the realtor's name?"

"I do, but they went out of business a couple of years back."

Another dead end.

"Never mind then. I appreciate your time."

"Uh huh." He tipped his hat back down to cover his eyes, and went back to doing nothing, waiting for the world to go slowly by.

Next stop, Bobby White's house. Maybe he had some information on her, if they were related. If not, it was back to square one.

Bobby White's house didn't look much different from the one he had just left on Orchard Street. There was certainly no Better Homes and Gardens issues in the future here. The yard was more sand than grass, and what few patches were there, had turned brown.

There was a back seat from an old car or truck on the porch to use as a place to sit, being guarded by a Rottweiler, who barely lifted his head when he noticed Dagan's presence.

The screens were long gone out of the windows of the house, but they were open anyway to let in the breeze, and whatever decided to crawl or blow in.

He carefully walked past the dog and knocked on the screen door. There was no answer, so he knocked again this time saying, "Hello, anyone home?"

From the side of the house came an answer.

"Hold your horses, I'm coming." A short, stout man came from the side of the house and around to the porch.

"Detective Murphy. Sheriff's department." He plainly stated sticking his hand out to shake the other man's hand. He was busy wiping the grease off, so Dagan lowered his arm.

"Whatcha want?"

"I'm looking for Bobby or Tammy White."

"I'm Bobby. Tammy's my sister."

"Do you know where I can reach her?"

"Nope. I ain't seen or heard from her in years. She run off with some guy leaving a note saying he was going to give her a better life. Last I heard from her."

"How about your parents? Have they heard from her?"

"Parents were killed in a car crash not long after Tammy took off."

"Sorry to hear that." and he truly was. He knew how it felt to lose a parent.

"What do you want with her anyway?"

"We are working on a case and her name came up as a person of interest."

"Must be an old one then. Like I said she's been gone maybe nine years now." He said scratching his head while trying to remember.

"You've never tried to contact her, just to see how things were going, if she was ok?"

"She left, not me. I figured if she had anything to say she would call or come home. If that's all you need, I have to get back to the truck I'm fixing. Owner will be around in a couple hours for it."

What an ass, Dagan thought. He would give anything to locate his sister and this man seemed as if he could care less.

Dagan thanked him for his time and went back to his own truck.

So, according to Tammy's brother, she had not been seen for quite a few years. The odds were getting better that he might have a chance at identifying the remains in the morgue. Tammy disappeared not long after his sister. Could the same person be involved in both disappearances? There was the connection with the bracelet. Tammy could be the girl that had stolen the bracelet from Regina's locker. That would be the only plausible explanation for her having it. This was one of those so-near-yet-so-far situations. The closer Dagan thought he was getting, the further out of reach the answers seemed to be. There had to be a way to connect the pieces.

His brain felt ready to implode. He decided to stop by the Reader's Attic, the bookstore Dani owned. He had to find a good spot to park his big truck because all of the older streets in downtown were parallel parking. A leftover from the past that was so nostalgic to Dagan. He loved the old town vibe.

Opening the front door, a bell tinkled overhead to let Dani or Beth, her assistant, know someone had come in. Dani appeared from the back room and smiled.

"Detective Murphy, it's a surprise seeing you here."

"I thought I'd drop by and see how you're doing. OK, OK, I lied. I just wanted to see your beautiful face."

"Oh gee, thanks." She feigned embarrassment.

"So, what's going on?"

"Nothing much. It's been slow today. What are you up to?"

"I've been checking out the names on the list we made."

"Find anything interesting?"

"Yeah, I'll tell you about it sometime."

"What about over lunch?"

"I was thinking more like supper."

"Well, why don't you come back after your shift and we can grab something."

"Sounds good. You here alone?"

"Yeah, Beth went out to take some packages over to the post office."

"Good," he said as he walked quickly around the counter and pulled her into his arms, giving her a long kiss. They never noticed the front door opening, or the tinkling of the bell.

They did, however, hear it slam shut.

Startled, they both looked up and saw Wade through the big front windows climbing back into his patrol car.

"Guess he knows you won't be accepting any dates with him anytime soon." He said with a chuckle.

"You think?" she asked as they both laughed. He gave her one more kiss, this time for goodbye, and told her he would see her around six. "Let me know if he gives you any trouble."

"He won't. He's a big pain in the butt, but harmless."

"That's what Eve thought about a snake once too."

Shaking her head, she slapped him playfully on the shoulder. "Get back to work Detective Murphy. The good citizens of Washington County depend on you."

She stood at the front door and watched as he drove away. She glanced down the street to the sandwich shop and could see it was getting busy as the lunch hour grew closer.

Tonight, she would order some food from them so she and Dagan could have dinner in her apartment. It was over the bookstore, and she just realized he had never seen it. Tonight, he would. She was over the moon. Her life was finally coming back together again.

This time she would not let anything or anyone stand between her and Dagan.

CHAPTER 17

The problem of trying to get birth records without a subpoena had been bothering Dagan all morning. If the sheriff found out he was looking into her past, as well as a child she had, there was no telling how she would react. He had known her all his life, but people could be like animals when they felt they had been backed into a corner.

There were so many questions about that child. Who was the father? Why was the kid put in the asylum? Why did she give him up for adoption? Sure, times were different back then in regards to unwed mothers, but Alice wasn't the type to let society dictate to her what she could and couldn't do.

Suddenly, Dagan had an epiphany. That little light bulb moment that every cop has that spins the investigation onto a completely different level.

The asylum had records strewn all over the floors the other day. What if the records were still being stored there? There could be records on this boy, records that could very well include a birth certificate.

He could feel his pulse quicken with excitement. He knew it was wrong, but he also knew himself well enough to know he was going to do it anyway.

After a brief stop in the McDonald's drive thru, he headed out on highway 77 towards the old county road that would lead him to the asylum. The same road that led right by his house. Funny how all these things seemed to be coincidental.

He finished eating his chicken nuggets and fries, washing them down with three big gulps of sweet tea, at the same time he arrived at the guard shack. This time, the guard didn't bother with his credentials, he just waved him through after pushing the release button to open the gate.

Once he parked and was inside the building, he explored the offices on the first floor. There wasn't much left other that what he saw the other day, just a few old rotting pieces of furniture.

The second-floor nurses' station had some files, but they were the same waterlogged pieces of paper he had found the other day. He rummaged through once more to see if any names stood out, but none did.

He realized that the attic might have been utilized for storage purposes. Great, the attic! Where every scary thing in every scary movie happens besides the basement. Thank God Florida didn't have basements. The high water tables in the ground prevented it.

Here goes nothing, he thought, as he made his way down a long dark hallway that led to the attic stairs. They creaked and groaned as if they were in pain with every step he took. He silently prayed that he wouldn't fall through them.

Reaching the attic door, he found it was locked. Every other door in this building seemed to be unlocked except this one. Nothing was ever easy.

Damn.

He wondered if it could be picked. He didn't have any pick lock tools, but he did have a debit card. It was an old door, and most of the older doors had spring bolt locks. He had read once that those doors are the ones that were easily picked by credit card.

He pulled his wallet out of his back pocket and got out his card. He inserted it in between the door and frame and jiggled it back and forth to maneuver it into the lock slide, all the while turning the knob back and forth. After a few attempts, it popped open.

Bingo, just like the movies.

The door swung open slowly with a loud but slow squeal, indicating it was long overdue for oil. Bright sunshine filled the room from a huge row of windows that lined the eastern wall.

Clutter filled every nook and cranny. There were plenty of unused hospital gowns and bed sheets in boxes, discarded furniture that had been put away in here for storage for one reason or another, and medical supplies and equipment that would never be sterile again. Along the wall to the left, there stood a row of filing cabinets. They looked to be solid wood, which spoke of their age. It was rare to see anything made from real wood anymore. None of these cabinets had locks, which was great. He didn't think his MasterCard would work on that kind of lock.

The drawers were each marked with letters of the alphabet, so he reached for the one marked with a B. He thumbed through file after file carefully perusing the first and middle names for the initials W.J.

He finally came across one. The name on the file tab was William James Baxter. That name itself wasn't familiar to him. But the name Baxter rang a bell.

He took the file and walked over to the row of windows so he would have ample light to read. Looking around he found an old wooden office chair on rollers and pushed it over to sit in.

He sat and opened the file. The first few pages were doctors' notes on the patient's entry date to the asylum and the diagnosis. It seemed the boy had a nasty fall at the age of 4 years and his personality went from cheerful child who loved to play to sullen and quiet, preferring to spend time alone instead of in the company of other children. His parents became concerned when he started showing signs of aggression towards other children, especially his younger siblings, and the family dog.

The last straw had been finding the puppy dead with the leash wrapped around his neck. The parents were terrified, so they placed him in the asylum to keep his from harming their natural born children. They also relinquished their parental rights back to the state since the child had been adopted.

There were a few pages that suggested the shock therapy they were using seemed to be helping the boy, and therefore would continue.

He just shook his head at the unbelievable. He skimmed to the bottom of the last page and saw the notes were signed by Dr. Joseph Baxter.

Baxter?

Was the child related to the good doctor?

He flipped through the rest of the pages to see if there was any information on relatives and there it was.

A thick piece of paper that had yellowed with age, folded in half. As he unfolded it, he had found what he was looking for.

Moments later, he wished he had never found it. He sucked in his breath. This couldn't be true! What he read on that birth certificate made him feel nauseous and he was glad he was sitting down. After feeling his mind reel back and forth for a few seconds, he stood up quickly causing the file to fall and scatter all about the dust covered floor.

Now he knew why secrets were kept. Now he knew why people didn't want others to know their deepest darkest lies. Secrets had the monumental power to shatter peaceful lives and destroy minds. This birth certificate would do just that.

Walk away Dagan, his mind screamed at him. Leave it alone.

He knew walking away would be easy, but he would never forget what he just read. None of it made any sense.

The boy had the same last name as the doctor according to his medical records. The birth certificate had the boy's mother listed as Alice Bayer, which had been the sheriff's maiden name. But the father listed was not the doctor.

The father listed was someone who seemed like a huge impossibility.

The name of the father on the birth certificate was Samuel Robert Murphy.

Dagan's father had another son.

Dagan had a half-brother.

CHAPTER 18

Dani zipped the deposit bag closed with the money from the cash register and the receipts from the day inside. She was closing thirty minutes early today so she would have time to go to the bank instead of the night deposit she usually used.

On her way back, she would stop by the sandwich shop and pick up dinner for herself and Dagan. She smiled at the thought. They had shared so many wonderful memories together, and she had ruined it by her jealously and insecurities about his work. Today though, she was focusing on the good.

A huge truck went by blowing its horn startling her and causing her to look up. She sighed heavily at the twilight creeping in already. She really hated the time change and could not believe the state of Florida was considering keeping daylight savings time year-round. She would be glad when it was time to "spring forward" again.

Although, this was a relatively safe place, she hated doing the deposit after dark. You just never know about people these days.

She gathered up her things, finding her keys in her purse. Locking the front door, she gave it a tug to make sure it was locked properly. Satisfied, she exited the store through the back. Her car was parked behind the building to give the customers the parking spots out front. She pushed the keychain fob and heard the *blurp* of the doors unlocking.

She opened the passenger side door and placed her purse, paperwork, and banking bag on the seat, closed the door and went around to the driver's side.

She started to open the door to climb in when suddenly from behind she heard someone approaching. She tried to turn to see who it was but was not fast enough. A rag covered her face while another arm snaked around her waist. The smell from the rag covering her face was suffocating her, and she did her best to fight off her attacker. It was no use, she could feel her arms and legs getting heavy and refusing to move. In her last attempt to defend herself, she tried to at least get a look at her attacker as she went limp.

It was no use.

Her eyes closed, and darkness surrounded her.

~ ~ ~

Shock was slowly wearing off and Dagan was drowning in a myriad of emotions. Confusion, anger, hurt, betrayal, just to name a few.

Did his mom know about this? Surely not. It would kill her. His dad had cheated on her and had a child with her best friend. A child that had been locked away in a mental asylum for children.

He had a half-brother. Rachel had a half-brother. Who was he? Was he still alive and if so, where did he live?

There were so many questions bouncing around in his head.

He needed air.

He quickly collected the papers he had dropped into a pile and placed them back in the folder.

He hurried down, out of the building and cranked his truck. Slamming it into drive, gravel spun up in the air as he punched the gas pedal.

He was going to get some answers ... today. He could truly understand the saying curiosity killed the cat, because he felt like he was dying.

His aunt had to have known this boy was her nephew. She kept close watch on him because of it, he was certain.

He hit the steering wheel with both hands trying to relieve his frustrations but it didn't do any good. He wanted to punch something or someone. He knew he could trust himself to go back to the office right now. If he saw Alice, he wasn't sure what he would do. All he felt for her right now was contempt.

How could she betray his mother like that? They had been best friends since high school. His parents had made her his and Rachel's godmother, therefore she had betrayed them as well.

The thought of having a half sibling the same age as him, left him floored. How different life might have been to have a brother. Of course, the kid had been confined to an asylum at a young age. He needed to find out everything he could about him and try to locate him. He would use every resource necessary.

Maybe he was doing fine now and was leading a productive life, or maybe not. His training in criminal psychology had taught him people that were troubled early on in life very rarely got better. Many of them became worse. Some could be controlled through drugs and therapy, if they stuck with it and took their medications responsibly. A loving and supportive family helped tremendously, but even that was not a guarantee. A lot of them learned to emulate acceptable behavior and managed to get by.

Some people were born bad, others were victims of circumstance.

He wondered which this young boy was. It probably didn't help that his adoptive parents had turned tail and run at the first signs of trouble.

So, here was this kid whose mother had given him up for adoption, his adoptive parents gave him up after learning of some sort of mental issues and was given the doctor's last name. Was this because the doctor had adopted him, or for some other reason?

Another secret yet to be revealed.

This kid never really had a chance at a normal life. Maybe he had, until he got that head injury, but after that, was anybody's guess.

How could someone throw a kid away? He understood certain extreme behaviors needed to be dealt with, but to abandon a child dependent on you, that he couldn't understand.

Aggression and animal abuse were serious. He would have been beyond worried if a child of his had exhibited those behaviors, but did no one love this child at all? Was everyone so terrified of a four-year old child they just locked him away for their own peace of mind? He found it so hard to believe his father could have allowed a child of his to be mistreated in such a way, unless he didn't know the kid had been placed there. He might have thought, or been told, he had been adopted by a good family and was living a normal life.

There was now a mystery of what happened to the boy when the hospital had closed down. Was he transferred somewhere else, or did a relative take him in?

There was the mention of shock therapy, so maybe he recovered enough that he was able to live a normal life again.

Dagan would never stop looking until he found the answers.

Now, he was not just searching for a missing sister, he was also searching for his missing brother.

CHAPTER 19

A dank, acrid taste filled Dani's mouth and nose. She struggled a bit to open her eyes, and for a moment, didn't remember what had happened.

Realization suddenly reared its head, and her abduction came slowly into focus. Confusion set in wondering why in the world someone would kidnap her. She had nothing other than her sales for the day. Whoever it was could've just demanded her money and left her unharmed. She tried pushing back the thoughts that would cause her to panic.

She pulled herself into a sitting position and looked around. She had been lying on an old bed frame with a thin mattress. She would rather not contemplate what the smells coming from it were, but it reeked of urine. Her legs were still shaky when she tried to stand, so she didn't trust them to hold her weight just yet. She sat back down, and wished she had some aspirin for her pounding headache.

Looking around gave her no clues to where she may be. This place, whatever it was, had long ago hosted its last occupants. There was a small window about eight feet off the floor. It was too high to look through even if she stood on the old cot. She didn't have the strength anyway. Thank God there was a full moon tonight. The light through the window lit up most of the room, as bright as it was.

As best as she could tell, the cot was the only thing in the room that couldn't be any larger than 12 x 12. There was a door directly in front of her. She knew without checking, it would be locked, after all, why bother kidnapping someone only to leave the door unlocked, right?

Her mouth was dry as cotton and she would love a few sips of water. Thinking about it only made it worse.

She thought she heard something outside the door. It sounded like distant footsteps. Her kidnapper might be coming back. What would his intentions be?

The footsteps grew increasingly louder so she knew someone was indeed coming. With each step, her heart pounded harder.

The doorknob rattled as someone attempted to unlock it. She heard the lock click and the door opened just a crack. She could see nothing but a shadow. A hand appeared and rolled a bottle of water across the floor, and as suddenly as it had opened, the door slammed shut again. The lock turned loudly, and the footsteps started their retreat.

She waited until she was sure whoever had been in the hall was gone. Lacking the strength to walk very far, she crawled across the floor to get the water. She fumbled with the cap, and once removed, she guzzled half the bottle without stopping.

It was room temperature at best, but it was wet. Waiting a few seconds, she finished it off.

Realizing it had been foolish to drink it all, she chastised herself. What if her kidnapper didn't come back any time soon? She should've saved half the water for later.

One problem at a time Dani! She needed to think and come up with a plan while resting to regain her strength.

She leaned against the cool dampness of the wall and tried figuring out where she was. She knew it had to be an abandoned building from the derelict look of the room. There were a few in town that had once been thriving businesses, but had long ago closed down. New and improved buildings stood on the outer fringes of town taking the place of the giant, well-built brick relics.

This room reminded her of a prison cell. It had solid doors though instead of bars. The only prisons in this area were fully operational. She didn't know of any that stood empty and unused.

The only other place she could think of that was similar was...

It couldn't be.

Terror seized her heart and gave it a tight squeeze. Could she be at the asylum? It was where those remains of the young girl had been found, giving Dagan all kinds of puzzles to figure out. Just this weekend he had found the information on the sheriff and her illegitimate child that had once been a patient here.

What in the world could be going on, and why was she being dragged into it? Did someone figure out that she knew, or that she and Dagan had information?

She had no idea how long the person that took her planned on keeping her here or what they planned to do to her. She silently prayed that Dagan had been to her apartment, noticed something had happened to her and would come looking for her, but how would he know where to look?

Her hope was he figured it out soon.

She didn't want to be the next victim of this place.

CHAPTER 20

Dagan headed over to Dani's place without being conscious he was doing so. He was on autopilot. He knew she could calm him and would be able to help him think rationally, to help him sort all of this out. Hopefully, she would go with him to see his mother. He wanted to talk to her first before he confronted Alice.

Since he was going in her apartment and not the bookstore, he pulled around the back of the building to park. Pulling up next to her car, he noticed the driver door open and the dome light was on. She must be unloading some things, he thought. She had said she was going to get supper from the sandwich shop down the street. She must not have been able to carry everything in at once.

He would help out by grabbing whatever was left. He walked over and peered inside. Her purse and bank deposit bag were sitting on the front seat, along with a small stack of papers held together by a paper clip.

Even though they lived in a relatively safe town, she knew better than to leave her purse in the open like that for anybody to walk by and grab. He picked up the bank bag, unzipping it and found some cash and receipts in it. Not only had she left her purse, ripe for the picking, but the bank bag too. Grabbing them both he closed the door. He walked up the back stairs to the door and tried to open it. It was locked. He thought it odd, but knocked. Several seconds passed with no answer, so he knocked again.

"Dani, open up, it's me." He said loudly.

No answer.

"Dani!" he pounded louder.

Still, no answer.

He took out his cell phone and dialed her number. There was no answer. He dug around and found a set of keys. He pulled them out and tried three different ones before he found the right one that unlocked her door.

He stepped through the threshold and called her name again. The apartment seemed to be empty. He could tell Dani lived here. Not one thing out of place, a testament to her OCD that used to drive him crazy. Now he realized it was called balance.

He was messy, she was a neat freak.

He was a maelstrom, she was the calm.

Where in the hell was she? Maybe in the store.

At the end of the hallway, that consisted of a bathroom and two bedrooms, there was a fourth door that had a dead bolt. Using the keys he had found earlier, he found the one that unlocked it, and opened it to a set of stairs leading down, that would take him into the bookstore he presumed. He quickly descended them and found the store empty, lights off, and front door locked.

He jogged back upstairs, pulling the door closed and locking it once more. He walked back through the apartment, grabbing her purse from the counter. He rummaged through hoping to find something that might give him a clue to her whereabouts.

He found a small notebook that had Beth's number in it. Dialing it, he had to impatiently wait through three rings.

"Hello?" Beth's cheery voice on the other end answered.

"Beth, its Dagan."

"Oh Hi." She sounded a bit confused.

"Have you seen Dani?"

"Not since I left at 3:00 for a dentist appointment, she let me leave early because she told me she was closing at 4:30. Has something happened?" her tone serious now.

"She not at the store, or her apartment. I found her car door open with her purse and bank bag inside lying on the passenger seat. Since she is nowhere around, I'm getting worried."

"That's not like her at all. I mean, where would she go without her purse? She would never leave the bank deposit like that."

"I know, that's what has me worried."

"Do you want me to help look for her?"

"No, stay put, in case she tries to contact you. I'll handle the rest."

"Please, when you find her, tell her to call me so I can stop worrying."

"I will."

They said bye and hung up. He then dialed the station asking for the sheriff.

"Sheriff Taylor speaking," she said answering the call.

Working hard to keep the anger out of his voice he said, "It's Dagan. Dani's missing. I found her purse and bank bag with her daily deposits in her car with the door standing wide open. I checked her apartment and bookstore. Both were locked and empty. I need a BOLO for her. Beth last saw her around 3:00 and Dani told her she was closing at 4:30."

"Dagan you know I can't do that. She's a grown woman and she's hasn't been seen for an hour and a half. She's not technically missing. Now, I'm sure she just ran an errand and..."

Dagan cut her off, "Ran an errand without her purse? As well as leaving her deposit for the bookstore

119

in a car with the door open? NO, I don't think so. Something has happened."

"Dagan calm down, we'll figure this out."

"Don't you, of all people, tell me to calm down."

"What is that supposed to mean?"

"Nothing, I'm just upset ... I need to find Dani."

"Dagan, you're a deputy, and a good one, start thinking like one. This is not time to let your emotions get in the way. This is Dani we're talking about, not Rachel."

That was an odd thing to say, he thought. He hadn't even thought to make a comparison to Rachel, but they both *had* disappeared out of thin air. He thought he might be losing his mind. This could not happen to him twice.

"I have to go." He said and hung up the phone before Alice could respond. A few seconds later, his phone rang and he knew without looking she was trying to call him back. He let it go to voicemail.

He was going to the only other place where he could find some peace long enough to try to sort out his thoughts and pull himself together. That was what he had to do if he was going to find Dani. Maybe she would show up on her own or call him. Her phone was not in her purse so maybe she had it with her. He had tried calling several times but she didn't answer.

He was going home.

Not to his house, but to mama's.

CHAPTER 21

Dagan could see his mother's Toyota in the drive, so he knew she was home. All the way here, as he was driving, he kept trying to think of the best way to broach the subject and tell her all he knew. It didn't seem there would be an easy way, other than to come right out and say it.

He saw her sitting on her porch swing. She looked so happy and peaceful, and he was about to tell her that Dani was missing and Dad had been a cheater that fathered a child with her best friend.

Good God what a mess!

He opened his truck door, and she stood up to greet him.

"Dagan, Not that I'm complaining, but what brings you by?"

"Come on Mama, let's go inside and have some tea. Maybe sit and talk."

"Fine. A glass of tea sounds just about right." She said with a smile. He put his arm around her shoulders as they walked into the spacious kitchen that had once been the heart of the home. He could remember family holidays, birthdays and Fourth of July bar-b-ques that filled this kitchen with happiness and laughter. Now it would be a place where secrets would come spilling out and tears would fall. They sat at the table where they had sat for family meals so many times in the past. Dad opposite Mama, Dagan opposite Rachel. She noticed the weariness on her son's face.

"Dagan, you look terrible. What's going on?"

"For starters, Dani's missing."

"What?" her hand flew to her chest. He told her what he had found, and about checking for her in the store and apartment.

"Where do you think she could be?"

"I'm not sure. I have a bad feeling. I think she was taken, just like Rachel."

"Dagan, you can't be serious. Your sister's been gone ten years. Surely whatever happened to Rachel, couldn't be happening to Dani. Could it?" suddenly she didn't sound so sure.

"There's a lot going on that doesn't make sense, and it all started with the remains of the young girl we found at the old asylum. We have Rachel disappearing ten years ago. We find the remains of a young girl, who may or may not be someone that went to school with her. The bracelet we found with her belonged to Rachel's friend Regina, who says the bracelet was stolen out of her locker and happens to be identical to the bracelet that Rachel had given her for Christmas. When I was going through the things in the attic to find Rach's yearbooks, I come across some things of Aunt Pearlie Joe's that had to do with the asylum, where the remains happened to have been found. I took them home and looked through them. There were pictures and medical records, notes, that sort of thing. There were quite a few pictures of one child in particular."

He noticed his mother pulling off little pieces of the paper napkin that her tea glass was sitting on. She seemed to be concentrating on it.

He continued by telling her that the child had fascinated him and he seemed familiar in an elusive way, even Dani thought so. He continued, "Dani was flipping through the journal that had notes of the conditions that the children had to live in and treatments they were subjected to. A letter happened to fall out of the back of the journal. It seems, if the letter is accurate, that Alice had a child out of wedlock. A little boy, she gave up for adoption, who later became a patient at the hospital. For some reason, Aunt Pearlie Joe took an interest in him, always checking up on him, keeping tabs, that sort of thing. I thought that was sort of odd, but with you and Dad being friends with Alice, I thought Aunt Pearlie Joe may be doing her a favor. The only clue to his identity were the initials on the back of the picture WJB. Did you know about him?"

His mother stood suddenly and walked over to put her tea glass in the sink. Then she walked to the refrigerator and took out some pork chops. She began unwrapping them so she could season them with spices. "I knew Alice had a baby. It wasn't easy to keep a child back then if you weren't married. I never told anyone because she asked me not to. Besides, it wasn't anyone else's business.

"I'm not so sure about that."

"How do you mean?"

"Who was the boy's father? Do you know?"

"She never did say." She would not look Dagan in the eye. She just kept busying herself with what she was preparing.

"Mama, I've known Alice my entire life. She is not the type of woman who wouldn't know who the father of her child is."

"She said she didn't know." She suddenly seemed deflated and smaller than her five-foot, five-inch stature.

"Mama, come and sit back down." Dagan said gently. He could see worry in her eyes.

"She said she didn't know," she mumbled again as she slid back into her chair.

"She did know. I found her child's birth record at the asylum." He thought curiosity would win and she would ask who it was, but she didn't.

Because she already knew, or she didn't want to know because she suspected.

"The baby's father was Dad." He reached over and took her hands in his.

"NO, NO, Alice swore, she swore that she didn't know." She spoke as if she was on the edge of hysteria. He stood then and walked over to wrap her in her arms. She was shaking so hard he was surprised he didn't hear her bones rattling.

"Dad had a child with Alice. A boy who was named William James. His last name on the birth certificate was Murphy, but he had been adopted then returned to the state and was given the doctor's name that ran the asylum. His last name was Baxter." She said nothing, just stared blankly at the wall.

He helped her stand and walk into the living room and sat her down on the couch. He grabbed an afghan off a chair close by and wrapped it around her shoulders. They sat quietly for a few minutes. Suddenly, Maureen spoke.

"I knew they had an affair. Your father and I briefly separated a couple of years into our marriage. During that time, I guess your Dad looked for comfort and found it with her. She was our friend, so I guess to him, she was the obvious choice. He said he immediately regretted it and admitted to me what had happened. She did too. They both begged my forgiveness and promised it would never happen again. I guess since we were separated, it didn't feel like he had cheated, even though technically I guess he did. I had just found out I was pregnant with you right before we separated, and I didn't have the chance to tell him. I didn't want him staying just for that reason, but I wanted to make it work because I wanted you to have a family. I knew I wouldn't be strong enough to make it on my own, or so I thought at the time. Your Dad and I worked it out, and not long after Alice found out she was pregnant. She assured me the timing was wrong for it to be your Dad's and claimed she didn't know who the father was. We both just accepted her explanation blindly because we wanted it to be true, not necessarily because we believed it." She grew quiet and Dagan knew her heart was once again breaking. She had endured so much loss, and now this.

"I'm going to try and find him. I don't want to upset you anymore than need be, but I just have to know what happened to him."

"I understand Dagan. You should look for him, he's your brother."

"I have to go now, I need to be out looking for Dani, but I don't want you to be alone."

"I'm okay. In the back of my mind, I always knew it could be a possibility that your dad was the father. I think I actually feel a little relieved to know the truth after all these years."

"I'm going to have to talk to Alice. It may not be pretty."

She placed her hand on his and said, "Do what you have to do son. These secrets have been buried long enough. You've lost your sister, maybe you still have a brother out there."

His heart was full of love and admiration as he said, "You're the strongest person I know Mama."

She didn't respond, she just hugged him tight. They stood that way for several minutes, just holding each other. What would he do without her? He knew he drew his strength from her and had learned how to handle the storms life threw at you.

He finally pulled back from her and told her he would stay in touch. He also asked her to stay put so he wouldn't have to worry about tracking her down as well. She promised him she would be there waiting and asked him to bring Dani home safe.

He told her he would. He couldn't do it for his sister, but he would not let Dani disappear from their lives like Rachel had all those years ago, if it was the last thing he ever did.

As Dagan left the driveway, his mom stood watching him from the window. The secrets of the past had finally reared its head, and now countless people could and would be hurt.

Although her loyalty would always be with her husband and children first, she felt a deep sorrow for Alice. She was a good person, and a good friend for the most part. She had always been a good godmother to Dagan and Rachel. Her pain had been deep when she had given her child up for adoption, and Maureen knew that pain had come from a mother's unselfish love, not some unrequited passion for Sam.

She knew her son well enough to know that he would not go easy on Alice, even though she was part of the family.

Not knowing if it was the right thing to do or not, she picked up the phone and called Alice. The least she could do for a lifetime of friendship, was warn her that a storm was headed her way.

CHAPTER 22

Alice never seemed to be at work lately, and Dagan knew she wouldn't be there now because of the time. She normally left around five and it was almost seven thirty. He needed some answers from her, by knew that the office was not the place to have that conversation.

He logged into his computer and entered Dani's number into a program that would allow him to see the last location that her cell phone pinged. It could help him tremendously in his search for her. As he waited for the program to work, he found a sticky note on the edge of his desk. He pulled it off the edge and read it. It simply said *find her – find me*. It was signed with the initials WJB.

Where in the world did that come from? He stood up and looked around and saw there were very few people in the office this time of the evening. He went over to the dispatch center and asked if anyone had taken a message for him. The two dispatchers Jamie and Darryl said no, there had been no calls come in for him.

Did it mean that if he found Rachel, he would find his brother too? Why would one have anything to do with the other? He was confused. To add to his confusion, he finally got an alert from the tracking program, and it came back that the last location her phone had pinged from was a tower about a half mile from the road he lived down. Her car was at her apartment, so how in the world had she gotten out there. He never thought to check if her car was working. Maybe it had broken down and she had asked for a ride with someone and they had taken her to his house.

He shut his computer down and headed out the door to his truck. The mysterious note would have to wait. He drove what seemed like forever. His house was dark on the inside, and he could see the dogs peeping out the front window just like they always did no matter what time of the day or night he came home.

He quickly unlocked the front door and called out her name. In the back of his mind, he knew she wouldn't answer, but he tried anyway. Where was she? He walked out on his back porch letting the dogs run out with him to relieve themselves. He looked all around but there was no sign of her anywhere.

He found Kojak staring off into the darkening woods again. Only this time, the hair on his neck was raised. Dagan looked off into the dense forest as far as he could see, which wasn't far this time of night, but apparently wasn't keen to whatever the dog was.

"What is it boy?"

Kojak looked up at his master and started whining. The whole world seemed to be losing its mind. First, his sister's case, second was the remains they found that had somehow mysteriously led him to find out he had a half-brother and that his boss was the boy's mother, now Dani was missing and his dog was worried about something out in the forest.

Dagan had an idea. He put Columbo back in the house, and pulled the door shut, not making the poor thing very happy. "Sorry buddy, I promise I'll make it up to you."

He harnessed Kojak and put his leash on him, found a high-powered flashlight, then walked out into the forest. "Find Dani boy. Help me find her." He let the dog take the lead, and Kojak was practically pulling him along at a fast clip. If she had her phone and had been in the area, maybe she was still out here. He didn't know why she would have been out here after they made plans to meet at her apartment, but that wasn't important right now. All he cared about was finding her. The report from the tracker program said it had been about two hours since her phone was last able to get a signal. Sometimes in these dense woods, cell phones didn't work. She could be lost or hurt.

A little way in, Dagan started noticing another well-worn path through the brush. It was further down from the one he had noticed the other day when he and Dani walked through the woods. It was not the one he normally used when he walked into the woods. Had someone been going through the woods that had led to the back of his property? Had this been where the peeping tom had come from the other night that they had seen looking through the window? Why would someone be watching him?

Kojak pulled and tugged as he struggled to go faster than Dagan could let him. He couldn't run near as fast as Kojak wanted him to. They had run for about three miles and Dagan was getting tired. He wasn't in top shape anymore. That was something he needed to work on.

They started coming out of the thicker part of the forest and Dagan was shocked at where he found himself. He was on the backside of the children's asylum. There were a few outbuildings that were for the caretakers, and some of the nurses that used to live on the grounds in a dormitory type building. They were crumbling and falling down but he could see the asylum ominously in front of them. Why had Kojak brought him here? He must have been crazy coming out here at night. He didn't like this place in the daytime.

Dani had been very interested in the case, and the things they had figured out the other night. Maybe she had decided to do some snooping of her own. He hoped not, because this place had become dangerous from the state of disrepair it was in.

Kojak led him onward to the back steps of the asylum. The door was not unlocked so they had to walk around to the front entrance. Dagan swung the front door open and it made the loud groaning noise that old doors make. It still gave him the creeps although he knew it was just what old doors do. Kojak sniffed around a few seconds and then pulled towards the stairs.

They had both started up the staircase when Dagan heard something. It sounded like a door slamming shut, but he couldn't be sure. He told Kojak to sit, and he instantly obeyed. He stood still and listened, but whatever it had been was silent now.

Man and dog continued down the dark hallways. His flashlight was military grade so it put out quite a bit of light, but shadows still hid in the corners where the light didn't quite reach. It did little to stifle the nervousness he felt being here, but he had Kojak with him for protection. From what he needed protecting, he had no idea. He also had his service weapon holstered safely in the back waist of his jeans.

They searched room by room finding nothing. He even ventured down the left and right wings that were offshoots of the straight hallways he had stayed in the other times he had been out here. He made it almost to the end of the east hallway when he came upon a locked door. There was a small slot about two inches high and about 12 inches long. His guess was that was for passing food trays through to whoever had the bad luck to be locked into the room.

Lord, don't let me regret this he thought as he bent down to take a peek through the slot. He held the flashlight up to one end to give some illumination to the room and looked in. It was devoid of anything but dust and rat droppings. There were two rooms left on this wing one on each side of the hallway. The one on this side was the same, locked and empty. He crossed the hall to the last door and his flashlight reflected on something. Getting closer he could see it was locked too, but with a new padlock. Kojak was pulling towards the door and started whining. Dagan inched closer and Kojak began clawing at the bottom of the door and jumping up on it. The whining then turned into barking. Something or someone was on the other side of that door. The question was who or what.

He had no tools to work with to pick the lock, but he supposed he could shoot it off, or at least try.

He pulled his gun out and told Kojak to sit. He guided the dog to the other side of the hallway behind him and ordered him to stay, in case of a ricochet.

Dagan took his gun out and fired and heard a small scream.

"Dani?" he called out.

"Dagan?" The voice sounded distant.

"I'm coming. Move away from the door so I can try again to shoot the lock off."

He fired once more and the lock broke apart. He rushed through the door, and Dani flew into his arms and burst into tears. Kojak joined the fray by jumping up and licking Dani in the face. She hugged him and Dagan ordered him down.

"What happened? How did you get in here?"

"I don't know. One minute I was unloading my car, the next I am waking up in this place. Someone came up from behind and shoved a rag over my nose and mouth with something awful smelling on it causing me to pass out."

"You didn't get a look at who attacked you?"

"No. I didn't. It happened so fast."

"I can't figure out what the hell is going on here. We need to get out of here. Are you okay to walk? I came through the woods from my house?"

"I think so. I'm a little weak, but I can run if it means getting out of this place."

They hugged each other tightly for a few moments from sheer relief.

"I'm so glad you're ok. You had me scared to death. Don't do that again, Ok?"

"I'm going to certainly try my best not to. I love you."

"I love you too."

Suddenly Kojak got between them and the door and started growling.

A familiar voice came out of the darkness.

"Well, well. Isn't this a cozy little reunion?"

Neither Dagan or Dani could believe their ears, until the figure stepped into the room. His face was illuminated by the lantern he carried so now they knew just who they were dealing with.

CHAPTER 23

"Wade, what in the hell do you think you're doing?" Dagan yelled.

"All will be revealed in time." He eyed Kojak and told Dagan, "Call your dog off or he'll be dead."

Dagan ordered Kojak to sit and stay. He did, of course, always obedient to his master.

Wade pointed the gun in his hand at them and motioned them out of the room with it.

"Oh, by the way, hand over your piece nice and slow. I heard shots fired so I know you have it on you, and your cell phone too."

Dagan removed the gun from his waist and handed it butt first to him. Wade tossed both items into the room and then shut the door, closing Kojak inside with Dagan's only weapon or means of calling for help.

He made them walk up to the third floor and into the autopsy room where the remains had been found.

"Tell me what you're doing Wade. This is ridiculous. You kidnap Dani, now you're holding us both at gunpoint? You're throwing your entire career away and for what?" Dagan asked.

Wade mostly ignored him and then instructed them both to sit in chairs that had been pushed together back to back. He took rope and tied up Dagan first, threatening Dani if he made a wrong move, then tied her up next.

"Once Dagan is gone Dani, we can be together," he said getting very close to her face.

"You plan on killing me?" Dagan asked incredulously.

"Why not? You can be with your precious sister at last."

"You know where Rachel is? What did you do to her?"

"I have no idea where she is, but I do know she is no longer breathing."

Dagan started furiously pulling at the ropes around his hands. He heard Dani gasp.

Wade wasn't making very much sense then he smiled the most evil smile that Dagan or Dani had ever seen.

"What do you mean? If you hurt her..."

Wade cut him off. "You'll do what? I told you I didn't do anything to her. You think I would hurt my own little sister?"

Dagan felt as if he had suddenly been submerged in water and was being held down by force. All the air left the room, and the silence was deafening. He was momentarily stunned into silence.

Wade was his missing brother? Denial screamed through his head. The initials were all wrong, weren't they?

WJB. William James Baxter.

Wade Jeter.

WJ, the B was missing. Could it really be that simple?

"I think I see some reality setting in brother. I bet you have so many questions. Didn't you find the note I left for you on your desk?"

"Yes, I found it, but it didn't make much sense. I thought it had something to do with Rachel. You're right though, I do have a few questions."

"It meant if you could find me, you would find Dani. I guess you're not so great at figuring out clues after all. Go ahead with your questions, I'll do my best to answer them." Wade hopped up onto the examination table that had recently been the center of their investigation and crossed his legs. He had the gun pointed straight at Dagan.

"Where is she Wade?'

"I told you, I don't know where she is. I met up with her after school all those years ago and told her the truth about her dad, our dad. I had decided that between the two of you, she would be easier to talk to, to convince. You were always such an ass thinking you were better than me. She seemed so sweet, so I thought she would be accepting of me as her brother. I was wrong. She freaked out. She called me a liar and said her dad would never cheat on her mom. Said she was going to get me in plenty of trouble if I spread that kind of gossip. I swear to you though, she left going to some dance or piano lesson she had that day. I never saw her alive again. You and I both know from working cold cases how most of them end, that is if they are ever solved."

"Why didn't you ever tell me that you and I are brothers?"

"After the way Rachel acted? You already hated me. I thought if she reacted the way she did, you would be ten times worse, so I kept it to myself, knowing that one day it would come in handy. Looks like today's your lucky day. I found out myself when I overheard my second adoptive mother talking to her sister one day. That's how I found out Alice was my real mom and I confronted her. She was happy to finally have her baby boy back in her life so she told me everything. She helped get me a job, and like the good son I am, I kept mommy's secret, so long as I got my way. How do you think I always got the primo cases?"

Dagan felt a miniscule pang of guilt and pity for the man he saw before him. This was the little boy in the pictures he had wondered about. The boy given up at birth, given back by his adoptive parents, confined to an institution, and from there God only knew what else. He had never shown him much in the way of friendship, but when he had, it had been rejected. Now the same man had a gun threatening both him and Dani. This was the brother he had so desperately wanted to find just a few hours ago, a man who he had grown up with as his rival. Suddenly Dagan was angry at the world for this situation. He could only imagine the depth of emotion Wade must feel.

"Look man, we can work this out. I just found out I have a brother and told my mom I was going looking for you. I've lost my sister, I don't want to lose you too." Dagan spoke calmly trying to diffuse the situation.

"Oh, so we can be one big happy family now? You're such a liar Dagan. You can't stand me and everyone knows it. It's ok bro, the feeling is mutual." Wade hopped down from the table and walked towards Dani. Dagan couldn't see what was going on with his back to her.

Wade knelt down in front of her and put his hands on her cheeks. "You and I will have such a good life together once he's out of the way." He licked his lips making Dani want to gag. He leaned in close and whispered, "We'll have our own babies, and they'll have a real family." He traced her face with his fingers, and then kissed her on the mouth, causing her to turn her head in disgust. He slapped her, and the smack resounded through the room.

"So, you're too good for me now? You were more than willing to go out with me a couple of weeks ago, but then Dagan finds out and is so jealous he had to try and win you back with the same old lies he has always told you. How do you go back to a man that threw you out like yesterday's trash? Have it your way princess. You can die with your loser ex-husband."

Dagan was working furiously on his ropes. He was going to choke the life out of him for hitting Dani like that. He could see Wade was truly delusional now. He almost had the ties undone enough that he could slip his hands out unseen when another familiar face entered the room.

The authoritative voice spoke calmly.

"William James, what do you think you are doing?"

CHAPTER 24

"Well, if it isn't dear old mother!" Wade exclaimed.

Alice stepped into the room carefully, never taking her eyes off Wade.

"Why did you take Dani? I told you to leave her alone."

"Why is that mother? So your precious Dagan could have her all to himself? He had his chance and he blew it. She's mine now, or was, until she decided to join him and Rachel."

Everybody could see that Wade was losing his grip on reality. His eyes looked wild. A dark energy seemed to be crackling and circling all around them.

Dagan felt his bonds fall loose. Finally! He kept his hands behind his back waiting for just the right moment. As Wade was arguing with Alice, he whispered to Dani that his hands were free and he was going to try to stop Wade. He wanted her to stay quiet and try to not to anger Wade for any reason. He waited for the moment when Wade's back was turned and leaped out of his chair, knocking Wade to the floor, startling everyone.

A fist fight ensued.

Dani was busy trying to free herself in case Dagan needed help, while Alice looked on in disagreeable shock. Since Dagan had taken Wade by surprise, he knocked the gun out of his grasp and it went sliding across the floor and out of sight.

Between the sounds of fists meeting flesh, and grunts and groans from both men pummeling each other, the tension in the room was palpable.

Suddenly a gunshot rang out, and everyone paused instantly. Alice had fired a shot in the air from her own service weapon.

"Get up you two. I have been putting up with this bickering nonsense from you two for long enough."

Dagan wiped blood from his lip, careful to keep an eye on Wade should he decide to throw another punch. His left ribcage was aching too. Wade had managed to get in a few good punches. He noticed Wade was sporting some cuts and leaning up against a cabinet trying to catch his breath, so he wasn't faring much better.

"I'm taking him into custody Alice, for kidnapping Dani." Dagan finally said between breaths.

"I can't let you do that Dagan. He has been through enough." Alice said as she turned the gun towards him. Dagan stared at her incredulously. "It's why I came here. To stop you both from doing something stupid."

"How did you know where to find us?"

"Your mom called me. She was worried how you would handle confronting me with all of this and she gave me a little warning. I traced your cell phone out here, as well as Wade's. You two aren't the only ones who know how to do police work."

Dagan shook his head in disbelief. "My mom finds out her husband fathered a child with her best friend, and she's concerned about your feelings."

"Your mother is a special woman."

"She had to be to put up with all of this."

Wade sat up and managed to stand although it was a struggle. "How nice for everyone to have had such a great life with family and friends. Meanwhile, because of all of you, I've been through hell. It's time I have a chance at a normal life. All I wanted that day was for Rachel to accept me, acknowledge me as her brother. Instead she got mad, called me a liar. You've hated me for as long as you've known me Dagan, but that's ok. Even my own mother didn't want me, so why would I expect anyone else to."

Alice looked horrified. "That's simply not true. We've talked about this. I explained to you why I had to give you up." Her eyes brimmed with tears that were threatening to overflow.

"Sorry *mother*, I'm not buying your story any longer. Why don't we go ahead and let it all out in the open. Tell Dagan what really happened to Rachel."

Dagan's head snapped up. "What is he talking about? Alice, you know what happened to Rachel? You've known all these years?" He felt sick to his stomach.

Alice looked nervously from Wade to Dagan and back again.

"Answer me dammit. I deserve to know. My mom deserves to know!"

Wade smiled smugly and began the story that would forever mar Dagan's soul. "Well you see big brother, Rachel went running to Alice to find out if what I had said was true. Mommy dearest over there killed her."

Dagan felt his heart stop momentarily. This could not be happening. He couldn't have possibly heard Wade right.

Alice held out her hands in protest, shaking her head. "It wasn't like that. It was an accident, I swear."

Fury roiled through every synapse of Dagan's being.

All these years.

Never knowing what happened, never knowing where she could be.

"Where is she? What did you do to her?"

Alice was reeling from shock. "It ... it ... it was an accident. She came to me crying, saying Wade had accused me and her father of an ugly lie. Her face ... she was so heartbroken. I couldn't stand to see her so upset. Rachel was very intuitive for a girl her age, and I think she knew before I could even answer her. I told her the truth as gently as I could, but she flew into a rage. She started calling me names. I couldn't bear to hear those words coming from her. She ran at me wanting to hit me I guess. All I did was put my arms out to deflect her and she fell backwards hitting her head on the edge of my coffee table. I tried so hard to revive her. I tried to get her to wake up." She was sobbing, and her voice had taken on a hysterical pitch. "She is buried close to you. Her grave is in the woods behind your house. The actual location is in a notebook in my desk. They are GPS coordinates."

Dagan was at a loss. His brain was in overdrive trying to comprehend what he was hearing. Finally able to speak, he asked, "Why didn't you call an ambulance?"

"I was scared. I had just been elected sheriff. I didn't know what would happen. I panicked."

"You cared more about your damn career than you did my sister, a sixteen year old girl that had known and loved you her entire life."

"No, I loved Rachel. I never meant to hurt her, I was confused. I hid her in my garage for a day and then realized what I had done. It was too late for her. I had no other choice but to keep it a secret."

"You and your secrets! Those secrets have caused a lot of damage that can't be undone. You let us suffer all these years."

"I'm sorry Dagan. I'm so sorry." She looked near to collapsing.

Dagan sneered in disgust. He caught something moving out of the corner of his eye. Somehow, Wade had found the gun and once again had it in hand. It was pointed directly at Dagan.

Alice turned to see what Dagan was staring at.

"Put the gun down son. Dagan has been through enough." Alice commanded softly.

"Dagan ... always Dagan. How about me mother? You left me to a family that locked me up in this place to rot."

"I never intended for that to happen. When I found out you were in here, I asked the doctor that was in charge to personally oversee your care and get you the best of everything. He had been good friends with my father, so he gave you his last name and seen to it you had far better care than any other child here."

"That's supposed to make it all right?" Wade laughed a deep chuckle. "Guess what, it didn't work!" I'm tired of everyone else getting what I deserve and should've been mine. It's time I put a stop to it." He raised the gun and aimed it directly at Dagan's chest. "Say goodbye brother."

The loud report of gunshot and Dani's scream broke the eerie reticence that had suddenly consumed the room.

Dagan waited for the pain to spread through his body, but instead watched as Wade crumpled to the ground. Cries and tears of relief came from Dani.

Dagan looked at Alice who was staring at her son's lifeless body. "I had no choice. He would have killed you Dagan. He was bad from the start, he never had a chance. I couldn't let him hurt you or those I love anymore."

Dagan went to Dani and untied her. She threw her arms around his neck and held him tight.

"Dagan, tell your mom how much her friendship has meant to me, and that I love her."

Realizing what Alice was about to do, Dagan turned to face her and said, "Alice put the gun down. We can work all of this out."

She had placed the gun to her right temple. "Some things are better left the way they are."

Dagan lunged towards her to stop her from pulling the trigger, but it was too late.

Alice's body joined that of her son on the antiquated asylum floor.

After the shock wore off, Dagan and Dani went to get Kojak, and left that place of pure terror and hell.

It was time to bring Rachel home.

EPILOGUE

** One Month Later **

Dagan and Dani sat on either side of Maureen, holding her hands as they looked upon a rose-colored casket.

Dagan could not help but squirm a bit. The chairs provided for them by the funeral home were uncomfortable, and the tent that had been erected for the family to sit under did very little to stop the heat from the sun's sweltering rays.

The sky was somber and looked like rain was imminent. Of course, the heavens should weep for him and his mother, and cry tears of joy to welcome his sister.

He and his mother had agreed that relief was felt more so today than grief. The two of them had suffered grief for years and had now moved on to a place of acceptance. Of course, they would never stop grieving her loss, but at least now, they no longer had to drown in it. The what-ifs and what-might-have-beens had been to put to rest, along with Rachel.

The days following the incident at the asylum had left Dagan numb. He would have never guessed that Wade was his long lost half-brother, or that Alice had been the one to take his sister away from them, and in the end his half-brother too.

Knowing that Alice had killed Rachel, albeit accidentally if Alice was to be believed, had been harder for his mom to accept than if a random stranger had taken her. She never had said so, but he could tell. It had devastated him too.

All the years not knowing.

All the secrets that were kept.

All the lies that were told.

Alice could've saved everyone a lot of sorrow and despair, but didn't have the guts to face what she had done. In a way, he guessed justice had been served. She served it to herself, but none the less, she ended up paying for her wrongs.

They had buried her and Wade side by side on the opposite side of the cemetery from where they sat now. Only a few people had attended, mostly the curious, and some reporters from the Panama City Beach news stations. He couldn't bring himself to even look that direction.

The only thing he could find to be grateful to her for was the note she had left in her desk that gave the coordinates to find Rachel's grave. Using GPS guidance, they found her wrapped in a pink and purple quilt that had deteriorated but had helped keep her remains together enough for DNA testing, and a cause of death to be discerned from her skull fracture. It had matched what Alice had said, so he guessed that was what they would have to believe. It had taken a month to get the results of the autopsy back and have them release her body for burial.

The test results would be in soon on their Jane Doe they had originally found at the asylum. They were pretty sure it was Tammy White, but had to wait for the DNA taken from her brother to come back to be certain. How and why those remains were put there would forever remain a mystery. He suspected that it had been Wade playing games with him. It was just like him to pull Dagan into something like that just to be able to reveal everything to him about everything that had happened. Wade knew the connection of the bracelet was just the way to do it. The bracelet was found in

Alice's desk. She had never turned it over to the lab for analysis.

The crowd that was here today spoke volumes about his home town and how much they had respected his family. He had spotted Regina in the crowd and was glad she was able to make it to say goodbye to her high school friend that cared for her when no one else did.

He hadn't really heard most of what the priest had said, nor did he care to. He knew everything he needed to know about his sister and would remember her in his own way. Her giggle when his football buddies would come to the house and flirt with her even after being threatened by him, how they would fight over the last soda in the fridge, racing each other down the stairs on Christmas morning, even as teens. Nobody could take that from him.

Maybe he could sleep nights now knowing just where his sister would be should he feel the need to visit her. She would forever be resting by his Dad's side, and one day, she would rest between both the parents who had loved her dearly.

People began to stand up around him. He had been so lost in his thoughts, he hadn't realized the service had ended. Mom and Dani stood placing the roses they held on her casket. He followed and lingered a moment then turned away.

People were approaching his mother to give her hugs and condolences, ten years in the making. He felt his cell phone vibrate is his pocket, so he excused himself. It could be work but he doubted it. Everyone knew where he would be today. He excused himself and walked over to the shade of a huge silver oak tree answering the phone. The number was unfamiliar.

"Detective Dagan Murphy."

"Dagan, it's Tony Giovanni."

"Tony, man it's been awhile. I don't think I've seen you since we were roommates at FSU."

"I know, but I heard about your sister, and I was calling to say I'm sorry."

"Thanks, but we're all relieved it's finally over."

"I know it didn't end the way you've always hoped, but I'm glad your family has closure. That brings me to my second reason for this call."

Dagan's curiosity was piqued. "Go ahead."

"I just finished working a case in Big Pine Key and I have reason to believe there may be some connections up in your neck of the woods. You interested?"

"Yeah, I would love the chance to work with you on something."

"Alright, I'll see you in a few days."

"Sounds good. Don't bother with a hotel. I have plenty of room at my place."

"Thanks man, I'll be in touch."

Dagan said his goodbyes and hung up. He joined his mom and Dani. They were both ready to leave, but waiting on him to finish his conversation on the phone. He put his arms around his two best girls and led them to the car. He opened the doors for them and walked around to the driver's side. He looked over the roof of the car towards Rachel's grave one last time. There was a huge yellow swallowtail butterfly that seemed to be dancing in the air above it. He watched as the cemetery workers lowered her casket into the concrete vault that would keep the water out in the damp Florida ground and said goodbye to her one last time.

"Welcome home sis."

❂ ❂ ❂

ACKNOWLEDGEMENTS

I want to, first and foremost, thank God for the abilities he has given me. I was worried when I had to leave my job, but he has shown me a way to still "earn my keep".

As always, my family and friends who have encouraged me and been just as excited, and in some cases (though you shall remain unnamed) more excited than me, thank you for your support and love.

A HUGE thank you to Lynn Cutshaw. You took the raw pages and found my mistakes. Did your pen run out of ink? Again, thank you so much for helping me out, and your encouragement to keep writing.

To everyone who bought the first book, thank you for your support and I hope you enjoy the second one just as much. If you do, tell others!

ABOUT THE AUTHOR

After health issues caused Angela Jarvis to quit her job as a Physical Therapy Technician, she decided to devote more time to writing, which she has loved since her early teens. Angela lives in a very small town on the southern edge of Lake Okeechobee with her husband, daughter, and several fur babies. She has a grown son who is a sheriff deputy in the Florida Panhandle. He is a good source of information about law enforcement. "I find that ideas abound in a small town," says Angela. "Watching and listening is where all my best ideas come from."

Next in the series:

THE TIES THAT BIND

Angela Jarvis

Truth will ultimately prevail,
when there is pains to bring it to light
- George Washington

Prologue

Tony Giovanni shook his head to help clear his mind. He had been daydreaming again about cerulean waters, palm trees, and a red head with a fiery attitude.

He had just returned from working a case in the Florida Keys, where he had met her. She was the sister of the detective he had worked with, and he couldn't seem to get her out of his mind.

But enough of that, he though shaking his head to clear it. He had another job to do. When reading the newspaper earlier in the week, a familiar name had popped out at him. It was the name of his college roommate, Dagan Murphy. It seemed after ten years of Dagan's sister being missing, they had finally found her remains, and could put her to rest. She was the reason they had met. Dagan had decided to go into law enforcement because of his sister, and the two guys had shared a room in the dorm.

Call it fate, coincidence, or whatever else it could be chalked up to, he had been planning to call his old buddy in relation to some cold cases he had been studying, and then out of the blue, his name appeared in the Tallahassee Daily Journal.

The case from the Florida Keys had some definite tie-ins with some cold cases in the Northwest Florida area, and he intended to head that way soon. He knew that he would need the cooperation of the law enforcement agencies in the area, and usually it wasn't a big deal with cold cases.

He was going to call Dagan and ask him if he could depend on his help, both as a professional and as a friend. Picking up the phone to dial the number he had found through law enforcement resources, he smiled, eager to talk to his good friend.

He had no way of knowing the Pandora's box that was about to be opened, or that it would have a profound effect on them both.

Chapter 1

Tony followed the directions that he had programmed into the GPS in his rented SUV. Never having been in this part of Florida, he found it quite daunting a task finding his way around. One could easily get lost in the wilderness landscape that was unlike no other part of the Sunshine State.

It was heavily wooded country with forest on both sides of the state road he was currently on. There were very few signs to go by, but there were plenty of dirt roads you could turn onto from the main highway.

No thanks, he thought. Those roads could lead to just about anywhere. There were probably shotguns and banjos at the end of a few of them.

He was a city boy, so this was certainly going to be an adventure. It wasn't something he would willingly sign up for, but he had a job to do, and that was certainly something he took seriously.

He was careful to keep an eye on the GPS for the exact location of the turn off to Dagan's road. They had both been criminal justice majors at FSU and had kept in touch for several years after graduation, but had lost contact in the last few years.

Tony had applied to the FBI academy after college graduation, and Dagan had returned to his home town and was working for the county sheriff's department. He had recently been named acting sheriff until one could be appointed. It seemed the sheriff that Dagan worked for had died under some strange circumstances recently. Dagan had promised to tell him all about it over a few cold ones.

According to the GPS, the turnoff he was anticipating was in five hundred feet. Slowing down, Tony could see it was a dirt road that had recently been graded. He took the turn carefully. It looked like something you would see in an antique store oil painting.

The early morning sunlight filtered through the trees in spots giving it a very ethereal glow. The tops of the trees on both sides of the road had grown overhead, forming an arch over the red dirt road. This wasn't so bad.

Up ahead he spotted a small doe on the side of the road. He slowed again, having been warned by Dagan, they had a tendency to jump in front of moving vehicles causing accidents.

Driving in this peaceful place gave him time to reflect on the case he had just been a part of in the Florida Keys. Several young women had turned up dead and some of the details of the case had caused a flag to come up on some cold cases he had in a database.

Once he arrived on scene and had a chance to talk to the lead detective Valerie Mason, he quickly learned her suspicions were headed in the right direction, but she suspected the wrong person.

Toni, along with another undercover agent that was posing as a pastor at a local church, were there to keep an eye on the suspect, who happened to be the real pastor of the church they had under surveillance. Turned out the good reverend had murdered several women because of their chosen lifestyles. He decided their sins needed to be punished, and in doing so he could save their souls. He had even killed his own daughter, who had become pregnant at sixteen, and the father of the baby. The man had truly been evil.

As he drove along this scenic route, it was hard to believe that kind of evil could exist in a place such as this. He had never given thought to living in the country, but this place seemed peaceful, and so far away from what he was used to, it would sure be a convincing argument.

Before he knew it, the winding driveway Dagan had described to him appeared on his right. He turned in and drove a short distance before the road opened up into a beautiful yard with an old-style Florida cracker house setting dead center with a wide wrap around porch.

Dagan's patrol vehicle was parked to one side. He couldn't help but smile. It would be good to see his old friend after all these years, and even better for the chance to work with him.

He honked the horn to alert Dagan to his presence, and shut the engine off. He sat there a moment to see if anyone would come to the door. He could hear the engine making popping and pinging noises as it cooled.

Suddenly Dagan appeared from around the side of the house on the porch and gave a big wave. He hadn't change a bit. He couldn't help but grin from ear to ear and saw Dagan doing the same.

Tony opened the door and hopped out to greet his old friend.

ABSOLUTELY AMAⰅING eBOOKS

AbsolutelyAmazingEbooks.com or
AA-eBooks.com

www.ingramcontent.com/pod-product-compliance
Lightning Source LLC
Chambersburg PA
CBHW050407030726
47503CB00006B/2070